A sensual portrait of Manet's last years,
and a vibrant testament to the endurance
of the artistic spirit.

Suffering from the complications of syphilis toward
the end of his life, Édouard Manet begins to jot down
his daily impressions, reflections, and memories in a notebook. Between healing respites in the French countryside
and holding court in his Paris studio, he finds inspiration
in nature—a cloud of dragonflies, peonies blanketed by the
morning dew—and in the ocean-blue eyes of his muse, Suzon.
Entranced by Suzon, he decides to paint his final masterpiece,
A Bar at the Folies-Bergère, life-sized—wagering his health in
the process. In this stunningly original work of historical fiction, illustrated with Manet's own sketches, Maureen Gibbon
offers an indelible snapshot of genius, illness, and the dying
embers of passion.

MAUREEN GIBBON is the author of *Paris Red*, *Thief*,
and *Swimming Sweet Arrow*. Her fiction and nonfiction have
appeared in the *New York Times*, *Literary Hub*, *Playboy*, and
other publications. Gibbon resides in northern Minnesota.

The Lost Notebook of

Édouard Manet

The Lost Notebook of

Édouard Manet

A NOVEL

Maureen Gibbon

W. W. NORTON & COMPANY
Independent Publishers Since 1923

Faire vrai, laisser dire.

—ÉDOUARD MANET

The Lost Notebook of

Édouard Manet

THE NOTEBOOK IS REAL—*Monsieur Manet gave it to me. A few weeks before he died, he bade me take it.*

I first met him over my ironing board when I cleaned some wax from his coat. He and Méry were at a fête, some big do for Bastille Day, and he had gotten candle wax on the tails of his coat. It was nothing to remove—I pressed the cloth between some clean rags, and the heat of the iron drew the wax right out. But he thought I was so skilled. "Ah, Elisa," he said. "You have saved me!" I laughed at his silliness but it was nice all the same. Nice to be noticed.

When he got so sick, Méry sent me often to see him. I brought candy sometimes but mostly flowers. Some days I stopped by on my own and took a sprig of whatever I found growing. Tansy, mullein, mallow, snapdragon—even thistle. He loved those common flowers, too. The weeds.

One day I brought to him a dead bumblebee I found on the ground. A furry bumblebee with see-through wings. He got so quiet when I put it on his palm, and he studied it for such a long time that I didn't know what to think. Then he said, "Gone but still glittering." He saw the beauty of it, and that made me glad I brought it.

I tried to keep everything just as he gave it to me. As you know, I cannot read well, but I still felt as though I could hear Monsieur's voice when I saw the pages. And anyone can understand the little drawings. So yes, I did look through all of it, many times. I admit that.

He was my friend and he trusted me. Write it down that way.

Elisa Sosset, lady's maid to Méry Laurent,
as told to her niece Mlle Aimée Sosset in 1912

THEY WERE JUST WORDS. Sounds in the air. Said to make a point but with no malice intended. They came from the mouth of an old friend. Someone I have known all my life, or nearly. Since we were boys. Now he is graying and so am I.

I told him I would consider the idea but I did not mean it. And yet here I am, writing in these pages, just as he suggested I might. After all my protests—

So why do his words stick with me? Did they strike harder than I let on? Than I realized? Yes, and yes.

You cannot paint everything. That was what he told me.

Of course. It only stands to reason. Logic. One picks and chooses how to spend time. And yet it meant more to me.

I can almost believe he said it in consolation because he knows I am going to Materne's clinic in Bellevue. He knows the days will be long and enervating, the results questionable. I believe he meant there are other worthy tasks I might undertake—he kept using the word "legacy." But you cannot tell people what to think. I found that out in '67 when I wrote my little catalogue for the show that no one attended—a manifesto that no one read. People make of you what they will. They compare you to others, or to what they want you to be. So I told Tonin what I always say: my work is the only legacy.

That was when he said it. *You cannot paint everything.*

I felt as caught out as I did that day on rue Amsterdam when the lightning pain came on me so suddenly and so fiercely I could not do anything. Except fall.

You cannot paint everything. The kind of thing only an old friend can say. Dare say.

Or maybe I have it all wrong. Perhaps Tonin said it not because he dared, but because he knows what I have been trying to hide. He said those words looking directly at me as if to say, *I have deciphered you.* He knows me, just as I know him. When I painted his portrait this winter, I painted him as an aging Christ going to see Mary Magdalene. Not the young man who seeks to preserve his purity and mission but the very human one who knows one must take his consolation as he finds it in this world. Only in this world.

As we once promised each other we would, my old friend spoke the truth to me. His words were true, and that is why I cannot let them go.

I cannot paint everything because I no longer have the time.

WE HAVE COME TO our rented house with our pots and pans and everyone in tow: Suzanne, my mother, Léon, and me. Even S's black kitten made the journey. He traveled in a basket, the lid woven shut with ribbon.

The first thing Léon did was wrestle an extra table and small bed into this back room overlooking the garden, which is to be my retreat— my library, my studio. So here I sit like a pasha, watching the unpacking, weighing in. But when Léon asked where I wanted the crates of painting supplies and the easel, I lifted my chin to the corner of the room. That is as much interest as I have in any of it right now.

How much simpler if I were staying in an apartment on the clinic grounds as I did last year! But things are different now, as everyone from Sireday on down has told me. As if I did not know—

As I write, S's new kitten sits inside the doorway. He watches all the activity, but if anything alarms him, he runs back to hide beneath my chair. I find it comical. Until today he was afraid of me. But in a new place with so much going on, he has decided I am not so bad. I can see him making his calculations as he dashes back. *At least the monster with the stiff walk is familiar,* he tells himself.

"ARE YOU READY FOR the waterfall, m'sieur?" M. Victor asked this morning when I showed up in the tiled room, as if he had seen me just the day before instead of six months ago. But that is his joke, at least one of them. All the attendants have such comments, and each man employs his repertoire variably.

Last fall the familiarity offended me, but now I see it is necessary. If the treatment were once-and-done, that would be one thing, but day in and day out, and for the second time in under a year? There is no chance at pretense. You cannot come slapping into the room, strip down, and then have a man shoot cold water at your legs, alternating it with massage and slaps and jiggling, and not become familiar.

"Let us hope I don't drown in today's waterfall," I said as I sat myself on his spartan metal chair.

"No, no. It is a fine day, m'sieur. Just sit here and enjoy my chaise longue."

He had turned on the water by then and began to point the hose at my feet and ankles. Then there was no need to talk. Once the hydropathic treatment begins, the water speaks for us.

What none of the attendants ever ask is *how I am*. I think the powers in charge must tell them not to. If I volunteer the information, M. Victor greets it with enthusiasm or commiseration, whatever is fitting, but he never inquires. Because of course the truth is all too clear: if we felt at all well, we would none of us patients be here. Instead we limp and slap our way into waterfalls and sylvan pools, where we meet with water sprites and mermaids, joking all the while.

Dr. Materne has me on a three-times-a-day regimen. Water hose and pummeling in the morning and evening, swimming in the afternoon. And while M. Victor and the other attendants are all fine people, all fine men, they are nothing like the women in Dr. Béni-Barde's clinic in Paris.

When M. Victor and the others lay their hands on me, I can pretend no illusion of a pleasurable massage as I did with the Béni-Bardeuses—the muscles of my legs and back are pinched and slapped and then rubbed vigorously between rough palms. It is a kind of torture, but it is a torture I signed up for, that I show up for each day, and where I greet my torturers by name.

When I am not receiving hydropathy, I take short walks, eat, rest, seek the sun when it shines. I live like a mollusk. But it will all be worth it to be healthy again.

UP EARLY THIS MORNING. I wanted to see the beds of peonies at the foot of the garden before the full sun of the day.

But when I stepped onto the second of the paving stones, the lightning pains in my left leg chose just that moment to increase. So I stood there, afraid to move forward or back. Willing my legs to hold me.

The kitchen girl must have looked out and seen my predicament, because in a moment she was beside me with one of the old deal chairs from the hallway. After I sat in it, heavily, she stood beside me, talking. About Mlle Ambre, how kind she is and how much she likes working for her, about the house and the garden, about her family in the countryside. She chattered long enough for me to collect myself, and when I was able, I stood. Coming back inside, I leaned too much on her. When I apologized, she patted my arm.

"I am a farm girl, m'sieur," she said. "Sturdy."

Why are people like that so kind? It is not just that one pays them. Many people are paid but not all are kind. The payment some receive for their work makes them defensive, while others in their hunger turn clever and cruel.

What would the world be if people like Reine (for that is the kitchen girl's incomparable name, Reine Piolet) were in power?

To live under such a reign—

IN PARIS THE KITTEN'S name was Jacques, but out here he is Jicky.

He sleeps now in a corner of my room, curled in his basket, yet how he fought to be free of the thing on the way out here! Biting at the ribbon the whole time, and trying to work his paws between the lid and the basket itself.

Now his prison has become a safe nook. The dreaded basket belongs to him and him alone, so he has decided to love it.

MLLE PIOLET BROUGHT a chair down to the foot of the garden and then walked down with me. She placed the chair in among the bushes so I can lean forward easily to sketch. As I was settling myself, she told me that once, when she was a girl, she peeled open a green peony bud.

"I thought the color the flower would be was hidden inside. Like a bead. When I saw that the inside was milky green, I felt so bad. I hid the bud beneath the bush so my mother wouldn't find it."

As she spoke, she held one of the peony buds between her index and middle fingers and ran her thumb over the green sphere. If I were to paint her, I would paint her exactly that way: staring down at the bud as she caressed it with her thumb and its rough nail.

After she left me to sit and rest, I did the thing I wanted to do since seeing the peonies—I pressed my face to the flowers. The petals were impossibly soft, softer than silk or a woman's skin against my lips, and they were still moist with dew this morning. Different varieties flower in the beds, but my favorite is a dense white bloom with several crimson petals at the throat. It smells as fragrant as a rose. But why even make that comparison? Something always loses in such comparisons, or becomes less than it is. The peony smells as fragrant as a peony.

The trick is always to be in love—Victorine told me that years ago. Not just in love with a person but with things. With flowers or colors or cats in windows, with anything you see every day. So I will be in love with peonies in the peony kingdom at the foot of the garden.

I WAS BORN 23 January 1832 in Paris. My father did not approve of my desire to paint, but I did so anyway, studying first with Couture—

My uncle Edmond introduced me to art, taking me to museums in the city, where we walked for hours—

What is the beginning anyway? The true beginning? Did it start in those rooms beside my uncle, looking and watching, or was something in me from even before?

I remember a blue book of poems that belonged to my mother whose color bewitched me. I remember always trying to draw a horse but it would never come right, looking like a misshapen dog or worse.

That was why the *carnets* of my uncle, filled with sketches that seemed so accurate and filled with life, mesmerized me. That he could look at a house or a tree or a bowl of fruit and reproduce it on paper—that seemed like a miracle to me when I was small. His carnets were the only books I truly wanted to read.

Then, when I was old enough, I spent Thursdays or Sundays with him, walking through painting-filled rooms, together much of the time, talking mostly but at other times in companionable silence. Other days I would go off in search of whatever caught my fancy when I was ten and eleven and twelve. If we separated, and if he did not come to find me first, I could almost always discover him with his "favorites," as he called them: Murillo's dejected little beggar, or Rembrandt's woman with her shining pearls.

If I teased him about either, he would have a reply ready: "She has kind eyes," "I like her patient mouth," "We are all beggars in some way," or, simply, "I am allowed my loves." He said these things from the side of his mouth, loud enough only for me to hear.

The day he got us into La Caze's rooms, it was I who had to tear him from Ribera's dwarf—he would have gone on studying it, oblivious of all around him. When we got outside, my uncle was silent for a long time and then shook his head.

"A man's face on a child's body," he said. "Not one of Goya's idiots, either. There was intelligence in that face. And joy. When have you seen joy like that? The smile alone with those nubs of teeth could break your heart."

What had he seen in the dwarf's face and mouth that I had not? I looked at my uncle as he spoke that day in the street, and I saw in his face what I always saw there: a slight smile but also something sad in the wrinkling around his eyes. It was a look I never saw on my father's face. I think it was that day I understood you either have a kindness of spirit or you do not. It is exhaled with one's breath or it is not. My uncle was kind in the way that my mother was, and in a way that my father was not capable of, even after all his suffering.

Maybe Tonin had it right. Not about the idea of *legacy* or what I hope to leave—I mean he convinced me about this endeavor, this notebook of thoughts, this record of days. I have not taken this kind of care in thinking about my uncle in—years.

I will try to say here in these pages what I cannot paint. After all, I must have something to do with myself.

TODAY TO DISTRACT MYSELF from the ice picks in my skin I thought about the lewdest things I could: the brunette who hummed when she took me in her mouth, the black-haired beauty whose thighs were covered with downy fur, the society woman who anointed her ass with gardenia oil, so that if I took her from behind I came away smelling of that creamy flower—

Bellevue   18 MAY 1880

I THOUGHT I WOULD paint out in the garden. The small drawings I have been making in this notebook made me think it might be pleasant. So I had Reine Piolet carry out my chair and then a small easel. I took out the box for plein air work.

We got everything set up, I arranged my supplies and my cane—and then I sat there.

It could have been that I wanted simply to enjoy the pleasant afternoon. That I was tired from the morning's hydropathy sessions. Perhaps it embarrassed me more than I was willing to admit having a young woman carry my things for me. I am not sure. All I know is that I did not have it in me to paint. I saw flowers I could have painted—shadows and angles and colors—but it was enough to see them. To notice them and think about them.

Surely it must be enough just to sit and watch sometimes?

I WROTE AGAIN TO Isabelle Lemonnier this morning, even though she has not replied to my last letter. Each time pride tells me not to write again, and each time I disobey.

During the time it takes me to write to her, I am diverted. I become the person I pretend to be on the page. In the days that I wait for her reply, I am hopeful. On edge in a pleasant way. I look forward to the mail arriving without seeming too obvious about it. I let myself daydream and create fantasies. When too much time passes without response, I grow resentful. I find myself making resolutions. Declarations.

Then I let myself forget my disappointment so I can craft a new note, upon which I may place fresh hope, so the cycle can begin again.

Bellevue   20 MAY 1880

ÉMILIE AMBRE, FROM WHOM we are renting, said the dense white peonies with crimson at the heart are called Festiva Maxima. They are like a woman who must have the fullest skirt at the dance.

If I do nothing else when Reine Piolet nestles my chair among the peony bushes, I sit and admire the "white bombs." I bury my face in their petals and inhale for minutes at a time, no longer caring who sees me.

THIS MORNING I LAY in bed, half sleeping, when I heard sounds in the back garden. Groggily, I went to the window, and that was where I saw Reine Piolet standing at the back gate with a young boy, who had a crow sitting on his head.

It took a moment for my eyes to make sense of what I was seeing, and then my mind woke fully and in an instant. I was still tucking my night-shirt into my pants when I got to the back door and opened it—at which point Mlle Piolet and the boy turned to look at the noise, and the crow lifted off and flew into the trees in the lane behind the house.

"I am sorry we woke you, Monsieur Manet," Mlle Piolet said, walking quickly toward me and glancing back at the boy. "It's only he wanted to walk along with me this morning, and his pet comes everywhere with him."

"Take me down to the peonies and tell me," I said—so she walked me down to the peony beds, got me seated, and told me the entire story.

The boy is Reine Piolet's brother, Jean, who is eight years old and who has raised the crow since he found it on the ground last year. At first the baby crow had blue eyes and a pink mouth, and they fed it bread and milk and cut-up worms. When it was young, it lived in an old hat of their father's, even after it grew its feathers and could get around. The bird was very bad at flying for a long time because it had no one to teach it except Jean, but somehow it learned anyway.

"Now she can fly away whenever she likes, m'sieur. I wouldn't keep her against her will," the boy said, looking down at the ground.

"Only she likes to stay with you, doesn't she, Jean?" Mlle Piolet asked. "You spend most of your day together."

The boy nodded solemnly.

"And have you trained your crow to do some tricks?" I asked, making my voice light and easy.

"She will come when I call."

"Most of the time," Reine said, taking the boy's hand and jiggling it a bit. "Isn't that so?"

Again the boy nodded, still looking down at the ground. Then he looked up to the tree where the bird had flown.

"Do you want to try to call her?" Reine asked.

The boy ventured a glance at me then, a quick glance.

"I know she might not come because I am here," I said. "But it cannot hurt to try."

A quick nod and moment to think—and then the boy turned to the trees. He pursed his lips and made his whistle, two notes repeated several times, the last one a long, looping sound. And after a tiny interval, we heard a gruff caw. The boy again whistled, the same notes with the loop at the end, and after that second call, the crow came out from its hiding spot in the branches. It flew to a neighboring tree where it could better see us. After giving the bird a moment to watch us as we all stayed perfectly still, this *petit* Jeannot whistled a third time, and the crow glided down to the ground, not twenty feet away from us.

The boy looked back at me with great happiness then.

The three of us watched as the bird strutted in the grass, back and forth, mostly intent on picking at things but also turning to look at the boy and, a couple of times, seemingly at me. And I did not know what was greater in me, the desire to watch the bird with its black plumage that shone green sometimes and sometimes purple, or to watch the boy's face, which was also shining.

"She does not trust you yet, m'sieur, but she does a little or else she would not be here at all," he told me then, never taking his eyes off his crow.

He and I no doubt would have gone on happily watching the crow go about its crow business, but in a little while Mlle Piolet said very gently, "Mother will be missing you, Jeannot, and I must work. Say goodbye and sorry to Monsieur Manet, whom you woke."

"*Suis désolé, monsieur.*"

"On the contrary, Monsieur Piolet. Thank you for introducing me to your friend," I said. I could tell from the funny face he made at his sister that I both confused and delighted him.

The boy hugged his sister goodbye, and then she and I watched as he ran to the gate, and as the crow flapped up into the air to follow him. That was the last image my mind filed away—a boy running and a crow flying just above him.

Bellevue   22 MAY 1880

A WHITE SPIDER WITH a pink stripe on its belly sat on the peonies today. How can a spider match a flower *so precisely*?

ÉMILIE AMBRÉ SENT OVER a piano from her manor for S. It is a tight squeeze in the sitting room now, but no matter—the amount of joy the instrument brings is worth having one less chair and table. S must be happy because she has been playing Haydn for me instead of her Schumann and Wagner.

The opening of Sonata No. 33 always washes over me like a wave, making me remember mistakes I have made. Yet it does so in such a way that one sees the inevitability of them, and they become bearable to think about.

I was bold once upon a time—

Bellevue   25 MAY 1880

IT TURNS OUT THAT S's kitten is not a black kitten at all—he is a black kitten *with hints of brown and maroon in his fur.*

How did I fail to see this before?

THIS MORNING I HEARD crying coming from the women's stalls, and I am quite sure it was la Dame L—. When I looked at M. Victor, his face revealed nothing. They give cold showers to the belly for digestive maladies, so what must they do for "women's troubles"?

All is to be suffered in this place where we willingly submit to our torturers!

GODDESS OF THE RED hair and cleft chin—I have not seen her for years and now I cannot stop thinking of her. Is it because I wrote her name in here the other day? Vic'trine, the way she used to say it. Hours go by when I remember not only her and time spent with her, but also painting her. *La ligne du nu.*

When I saw her last, for Gare Sainte-Lazare, she was a woman, not the girl I knew. Yet when we embraced, it all came back. She must have felt it, too, because for a moment she kissed me the way she always had, and when we parted, she told me, *You taste the same.*

What I want now is what all old men want: to be young again. What I want is what all sick people want: to have my body back. Not memories of things, but a woman's body before me on a bed, frank and open—

WHEN I STOPPED AMONG the peonies this morning, I saw how many petals they had dropped, and how some of the flowers' edges were curling and yellowing. Seeing them made me think of poor Jeanne Duval, Baudelaire's mistress. She insisted on her impossible white crinolines for her portrait—even though she had difficulty walking, even though the ruffles were tatty, even though her foot had begun faintly to rot.

"I revel in the smell," B. told me when I started the thing. "If one truly loves a woman, one loves her stench as well."

That was before he decided he hated the way I painted her.

He believed I had not done justice to her, had purposely made her look "imbecilic." But I painted her face as best I could in the time she gave me. She was beginning to go blind, and now I think even sitting there with her foot up on an ottoman was an agony. That was the look I saw in her face. Not arrogance, as I thought at the time, nor the impersonal mask of a doll. Just a woman in pain.

JEAN PIOLET CAME this morning. His crow is called Lucette. She still will not fly to him in my presence, but she came much closer than she did the other week. Her eye is a glossy black bead, and she has feathers that grow down over her beak.

Jeannot and I talked for twenty minutes about her habits and practices before he got chased back home so he could help his mother in the garden.

WHEN I SAT DOWN to write to Méry today, I thought I would put a shine on things. But when I picked up my pen, I could not help but write, *Méry, I am doing penance here as never before. Though what I go through here is much worse than what the old priests used to give—I would say Hail Marys and all the Stations of the Cross each day if it meant anything.*

And even though I did not write any more about my malady, it was a relief to say that much, to say something genuine. I do not know what it is about Méry, but I do not mind if she knows I am suffering. I think it is her own vitality, her own spirit—one does not feel as if one is weighing her down. Her sympathy never cloys, and there is no need to keep up a brave front as one does with a man—as I do even with Tonin.

Do I feel love for her because she never broke my heart and I never broke hers? Or because she never demanded anything of me—except pleasure? The first time I made love to her she commanded me, "Now you wait. You wait for me." And so it was every time after.

Maybe it is Méry's own queer trajectory in life. Her mother thought the best way to give her daughter a solid start in life was to sell off her virginity to her employer, an old army general. Méry used the annuity a year later, when she was sixteen, to leave home and become an actress in Paris. She also began acquiring a vast knowledge of people and places, high and low, and where the wheel of fortune may stop. You do not mind when someone like that knows you, or knows about your pain, because they have seen so much.

In any case there is no way I can pretend with Méry—I had to ask her to handle the business with Barroil, who is her friend, and to do it quickly. I need money desperately, and those café paintings will bring a bit of cash. If confiding my dire financial state is not proof of real intimacy between us, I do not know what is.

This *carte de visite* of Méry Laurent by Paris
photographer Disdéri, 8 boulevard des Italiens,
was tucked into the notebook at this spot.
—A. Sosset

LAST NIGHT I SLEPT heavily for the first time since we came here— slept with closed fists, as they say.

Perhaps it was exhaustion, or some altered state. Because even when I did wake to piss, it was only enough to pull the chamber pot between my legs as I sat on the edge of the bed, and then I went immediately back to sleep again. Almost as if my cock and bladder woke and not my mind or thoughts.

What does it mean that the pain has stopped? I do not want to remember it or even think about it too heavily or in any great depth, since imagining can bring feeling.

Will I live in fear of my own thoughts now, for dread of pain returning?

I do not believe so. If anything, I have learned that the worst pain never comes when I think it will, and never returns in the exact same way. You go to bed with one pain and wake up with another. It wears as many disguises as a masker at a ball.

I AM STILL SHAKING a bit as I write this.

I have been feeling so much stronger that this afternoon Léon and I set out to walk to the river. We had only gone a little way when dragonflies—dozens at first, then hundreds—began to fly beside us. But even that is not accurate. The dragonflies circled us and hovered beside and above us. They were everywhere at once, moving as we moved.

I mean we walked inside their mass. We were *inside* some ancient, secret rite.

From time to time, one would light upon us—on our shoulders or on our hair. One landed on my face, on my cheek above my beard, and it stayed there long enough for me to feel the scratching of its feet on my skin and an almost imperceptible tic as it lifted off me and flew on.

I might have been startled, but I was too intent on feeling the sensation of the dragonfly's threadlike feet to be startled. When I looked at Léon, I could see the same expression on his face as I imagined was on my own. And it took me a moment to recognize what I was seeing in his face, to know it by its name.

Awe.

We walked slowly, looking up and around us, utterly silent. There was a density to the dragonflies because of their number, but it was not density in its usual sense because of the vastness of the sky, and because the dragonflies themselves were almost weightless and ever-shifting in the light. Their slender forms, dark and glinting by turns, went up and up into the blue sky until they were not discernible.

Those flying needles stayed with us as we walked along the path. I mean *they accompanied us*, the whole mass moving as we moved. As time passed. And we were inside the circling and the darting and the flashing.

One can paint a moment or time of day. Even the feeling of a moment.

It is what Impressionism is—the painting of a moment. But how does one paint movement itself? Paint time passing?

Or maybe I have it all wrong. Maybe what I need to do is paint the sensation of being in the same air as the dragonflies. So many wings glittering, catching the late angle of the sun, weaving about and rising up above two figures on a path—

I need to try. Even if I fail, the failure will mean something. One never believes that in youth—only age shows you that your artistic failures have merit, too, if only because they are records of days that never come again.

WERE THE DRAGONFLIES AWARE of us? They must have been. They kept circling us, they kept pace with us. The one that landed on my face did not behave as if it were alarmed—I think it was simply curious. Or else it just bumped into me. I can still summon the sensation it made on my skin—

Could they have wanted to communicate something to us, something we could not understand?

They come into the garden sometimes, after the sun is high in the sky. Sometimes one stays still enough for me to study, at least from a distance and for a moment. But that is not at all what I mean to depict. I want to show a *mass* of dragonflies, and what it felt like to be inside that cloud.

In one way, the idea is no different than the painting I did of S and Eugénie with the swallows at Berck-sur-Mer. One knows the painting is of a moment in time. One knows that in another moment, the swallows will have moved on in their swooping dance. I painted the swallows so imprecisely that the paint itself conveys their movement. But the viewer trusts in the optical illusion of the painting because they want to believe they can see the swallows in the air of the painting.

But to show the swallows circling the figures over time? Or dip-diving for bugs above the water the way they do here, passing back and forth over the river, the same group of them, for minutes at a stretch?

The problem would only multiply with the dragonflies, which were above us in the dozens, and in the dozens of dozens. The effect they created was not down to a single dragonfly, or even a small group of dragonflies, and it went *on and on*. That was the strangeness of it, and the mystery we felt we were privy to: the experience of being inside and alongside that glinting mass for a quarter of an hour. How does one paint sharing the evening air with them—the extension of the moment, the experience of time going on?

I think it must be impossible. *But I have not decided that.*

I SUPPOSE IF I am to say something about the start of things I need to say something about the sea voyage to Brazil. The years have blended the days together, but I can still call to mind any number of specific events and people. Besson the captain, and Lacarrière, of course, but today I am thinking of the barber who had worked for a time on a British boat and called us student sailors the English word "boi." How odd that syllable sounded!

He had a tattoo of a mermaid on his forearm—a crude thing, more a child's drawing than anything else. The chin of the mermaid jutted out, and she sported strange fins and scales, more like those on a flying fish than a temptress of the sea. Her arm-fins were sickle-like, and in one she held a small mirror.

But the tattoo I liked best belonged to the brutal first mate of the voyage, *un vrai loup de mer* who took pleasure in laying his hands on us whenever he saw fit. And yet someone loved him, for on the back of his hand was a heart pierced with arrows and these words above it:

PAUL RENTRE À TOINETTE

I will ask Eugenie to write to Léon and tell him where she saved my shipboard letters. He can bring them when he comes on the weekend.

LÉON BROUGHT MY LETTERS from the *Havre et Gaudeloup*. Poring over them, I recall the events and impressions in them, but it is as if I am hearing about them from a stranger. I do not remember *writing* most of what I read, except in a general way—but it is the voice that astounds me most. That I told my mother, in detail and often day by day, about what I saw and lived through. That at sixteen, I wrote to her with such love, with such a desire to communicate.

Yet even as I write that it seems foolish to wonder at it. Of course she was the one I most wanted to tell my stories to. She was my love—

So I reacquaint myself with dusty pieces of my past:

~ Once I learned, the pleasure of sleeping in a hammock, especially in the equatorial heat. Sleeping midair.

~ The strange whistling of the ropes and the mountains of seawater during a storm.

~ Seeing birds so far from the coast, including the little terns I saw at Boulogne. Like old friends.

~ Using a bottle with a red cap to catch a tuna.

~ Playing dominoes with the other students and the endless idle chatter about nothing. Days that went by without anything happening.

~ Seeing the phosphorescence of the sea, night after night, and singular nights when the glow was so bright the ship seemed to be cutting a path through flames.

~ Watching porpoises spin through the water, each like a flash of lightning.

~ Oranges, oranges—how much we craved them! And we could not stop in Madeira, nor at Santa Cruz, to replenish our supply, so they became like gold to us.

~ I was once near the shores of Morocco.

~ On January 6, the whale that jumped and breached, and the prodigious water it spouted. It was a monster, able to rise up almost entirely out of the sea, showing us its strength and otherworldliness. In the days that followed, I daydreamed of the depths it must have swum.

~ The flying fish that one day landed on the bridge, where we could examine its "wings." A slender fish-angel.

~ To be warm in January once we crossed the Tropic of Cancer. So much so that we filled a barrel each night with seawater and bathed in the dark.

~ Witnessing the sea become a "calm dish" when there was no wind. Days spent in the doldrums where we all prayed for a storm to move us out of that flatness.

~ Two sharks that followed the ship for a day but did not want to take our bait. Were they as curious about us as we were about them?

~ Crossing the equator and meeting King Neptune. The ritual of the performance. After, we students talked for days about who among us would be so bold as to get the turtle tattoo which we so rightfully earned.

~ The joy of entering the harbor of Rio, where my first desire was to drink fresh water! Where Jules Lacarrière and I wandered the streets and were pelted with the little waxy lemons by women on their balconies during Mardi Gras. Where I saw many pretty, simpering faces yet spoke to so few.

~ Rio, where I was bitten by a snake. Where I let myself think of the abuse I endured on the ship from the brutal first mate. Where I felt my loneliness most keenly, since it seemed to me I should have been happy to have such an adventure—and I was, but not nearly enough to account for all the misery. Where I ate my fill of bananas, oranges, and pineapple in hopes of storing up those good tastes for the journey home, the journey home. Where all the talk was of California and gold, and how the price of a bottle of beer was 150 francs but it did not matter because the gold was so plentiful. And how, even though it was said to be a famous opportunity to make a fortune, I did not think once of going because I wanted to return to Paris.

~ Rio, where I decided I would never be a sailor even if I could pass the test, no matter what my father said or did not say. Who was the young boy who acted with such bravado? I cannot remember being that way, and yet I must have been, for I lived through those months at sea and came home and declared myself. Yet that is what youth is. If one were to know of all the trials to come, the places where one can go wrong or choose badly—

But at seventeen, certainly after that voyage if not before, I did know myself, and I made the choice I had been making since I was a boy. I chose to follow my uncle with his magical carnets. I chose the company of color and painting, or they chose me. And if I took anything away from that long sea voyage it was the look of the endless ocean with its green waves and living waters.

Is this also part of what Tonin had in mind? I spent the last two days with these old pages, thinking of the sea and fish and sailors and oranges, ports missed and ports made, and not much at all about my leg. If for no other reason, this notebook is a success because it distracts me. Because it helps me pass the time.

JEAN PIOLET LET ME borrow one of his treasures overnight so I may sketch it—the bottom beak of a crow that he found in the woods.

The thing is a perfect V-shape, charcoal-gray with dirty, white bone ends. Each end has a small hole in it—where muscles attached it to the crow's skull, I am guessing. The charcoal tip looks like nothing so much as fish scales, or the layers in a fingernail.

JEAN PIOLET CAME THIS morning to pick up his bird's bill, and I made some little sketches of Lucette. When I had a few on a page, I let him pick the one he liked best, and that was the one I inked.

Upon my presenting it to him, he studied it for a long time. He then turned to me, and with great seriousness said, *It looks a lot like her, monsieur.*

I thought I understood him perfectly. I believe he meant that my little ink sketch was a good approximation of reality—which is exactly how we appraise art when we are young. We want our horses to look like living beings, a loaf of bread to look edible, and a woman's dress to look like satin. We want a painting or a sketch of a thing to replicate it faithfully. The closer a work of art is to reality, the greater the power of the artist. And all of that is perfectly acceptable and right—in children.

To Jeannot Piolet, a thoughtful critic.

THE WHOLE HOUSE IS sleeping in the heat. My mother upstairs in her room, and S lying on the divan in the sitting room.

Just now when I looked in, the kitten lay on the cushion behind S's head. Front paws in her hair, as if he had been braiding the strands—

WHEN I WROTE TO Isabelle Lemonnier again last week, I put a little watercolor of Jicky at the top of a page. This time she replied immediately to my letter, saying, "I adore your kitten. What a magnificent creature!"

Apparently my words on their own mean nothing. I must send a cat to do my bidding.

Needs must. Once started, one can have no shame in such things—I have known that for a long time. The main thing is that she replied and gave me leave to write as much as I like, and "to send such little things to please."

Very well, Mlle Lemonnier—I will play.

Méry says that I am foolish about women. That I can be bewitched by a collarbone or the angle of a hat. She says it as if it were a weakness, and yet it is no great task to remember people—the challenge is in forgetting them and allowing one's self to *go on*.

Right now I love Reine Piolet's hands with their square fingernails. The way she wipes them with a towel, or her apron, or simply on her skirt before she comes to help me with something I stupidly cannot do for myself. I believe I began to notice her hands that day in the garden with the peony, and now I cannot help but stare at them each time she comes near. I somehow believe I *can imagine her body* based simply on her hands.

Even with S it was true. All those years ago—a lifetime ago—when I was a naïve boy and a virgin, I still had such a sense of her when we sat together at the piano for my lessons. I had never been so close to a woman for such long periods of time, and her very presence captivated me. Sometimes when she sat beside me, her skirts would pull tight, and I would imagine how her legs might look based upon that tightening of the fabric and what I could see of her forearms. I drove myself mad thinking about the warmth between her thighs, and I wanted nothing so much as to slip my hand between those columns—

I will trace another kitten in today's letter to La Belle Isabelle and add in a swallow. Let us see what she makes of that.

THIS MORNING IN THE pool I saw it. The vision came to me so clearly I am not sure why it took me so long to understand.

I swam along as I always do, trying to let only my legs propel me. When I looked in front of me, I saw the entire surface of the water glinting with light from a side window. The water in turn reflected up to the ceiling and onto the west wall. The effect surprised me so much I stopped in mid-stroke and stood and looked. Three surfaces in the room shimmered with coins of light—and just like that I saw how to paint the dragonflies.

If I am to render the feeling of being in the air with them, I need to create a hallway of canvases. On either side, yes, but also above, suspended overhead. Large enough and high enough that the feeling of air is captured within the structure, and with a gap between the ceiling canvas and the sides so light can enter.

Absurd, absurd—but is it? Is it any more ridiculous than how they hang paintings at the Salon now, one stacked above another, up to the ceiling?

For a while I wondered at myself—why did it take me so long to see it? I know it happens that way sometimes—the vision comes whole and in one piece. But then I stopped and noticed the angle at which the sun was entering the window: it was at the very edge of the pane. Sometime over the past two days, which were cloudy, the sun must have shifted just enough in its path to shine through and turn the pool into a shifting mirror.

I felt better when I understood that. Spent the remaining time daydreaming of colors, and ways to paint shining wings—

I WROTE THIS MORNING to Eva Gonzalès. I think it may be the first letter I sent since the one in which I accused her of not seeking my counsel any longer as a mentor because of my lack of success.

I would like to say that it astounds me now that I penned such a thing—but it does not astound me. That year was as bad as any—another rejection from the Salon committee, and the portrait of Faure hung so high up the position itself was an insult. When I wrote to Eva the sting was still sharp, and my words to her were a recrimination. I felt she, too, had deserted me.

Yet what student does not leave behind a teacher? Amiably or not so amiably—but that is the goal: to one day be independent. How I used to castigate Couture for his brown sauces and trumped-up scenes—I was eager to dismiss him, to dismiss everything about him. And yet I did learn from the man. About the immediacy of the sketch, about the unity of feeling that comes from seeing quickly. And it was Couture who took us out into the streets after the bloodbath, who insisted we take our carnets and go to Montmartre to see the bodies.

"It is your history," he said. "It is your Thermopylae. It is your *Massacre of Innocents*. It is also a chance to study anatomy."

Eva did the one thing she could do: she moved out of my reach. What a dismal teacher I would have been if my pupil had not had the temerity and skill to do so. Yet I chose to take it personally, and to make it unpleasant.

Couture—I never did apologize to him. Never thanked him. Not directly. And yet I did in my own way. I railed against the romanticism and allegory of his boy with the soap bubbles, and then I turned around and painted Léon with the same motif. To be sure, I did not plant any symbols or hidden words, but still—it was a painting of a young boy blowing bubbles, and it was a nod to my old teacher, my old whipping boy.

Eva G. only did to me what I myself did to Couture. It is the natural order of things. If all the students would rise up against all the teachers and claim their right to the new—but how it does rankle to be the "old," to be the one who is no longer courted. To be the one that no one tries any longer to please.

LA LEMONNIER LIKED THE calico kitten and the "pretty bird." She is "constantly surprised by how charmingly" I can paint, since I scraped off and restarted portraits of her "so many times" it made her wonder "what was lacking."

I read the letter a couple of times to make sure I understood her assessment and accusation. Then I swallowed whatever pride I still have in order to respond.

This time I traced some old sketches of her onto my writing paper. They all show her neck and hair, and the dark tendrils she lets gather at her nape.

Do you remember when I kissed you here? I wrote in the space beside her neck and hair. *If I had to begin your portraits several times, you should forgive me. I was distracted.*

And signed my name.

I WROTE TO TONIN last week to say I had been thinking incessantly about women, even though the closest I get to any is when Reine Piolet carries my chair for me to the garden, or when I find ways to watch her hanging clothing in the side yard or washing the front stairs. *Like every old man, every old crust*, I wrote. *I am no different.*

He replied in typical Tonin-fashion: "Of course you are no different from other men. You are sick, not dead, and still hungry for another meal."

So it does not matter that I am here at Materne's clinic for a venereal malady—desire continues.

LÉON HAD TROUBLE FINDING my old carnets from Italy in the new studio, but this weekend he brought them. And the drawings are there as I remembered them: sketches of a Magdalen in a church in Florence who, inexplicably, has Reine Piolet's hands.

But it is not inexplicable, because people occur over and over. Not in the same city, not in the same lifetime, but over centuries. Reine is a Magdalen carved in the fifteenth century, Eva G. is Goya's *maja*—it goes on and on. Faces and bodies echoing each other over time. If we could wait long enough and travel far enough, we would each meet our twin.

That day with the peonies, I knew I had seen Reine's hands—the strong thumb with its squared planes, the long, final phalange.

Méry is right—I am foolish. I love knuckles and boots and hats and locks of hair. But it is not just in women. I painted Léon with his fuzzy little boy's hair in the portrait with the sword. How I loved to feel the soft, bristling burr against my lips when I kissed his head. Each time I looked at the painting, I could feel the sensation on my skin.

I should have kept it or bought it back when Febvre took it to Durand-Ruel. But the money was needed for something else, so I let it go. One cannot keep everything—

THE WEATHER IS SO fine I have been going out to paint in the garden these last few days. That sounds simple but it is not. Mlle Piolet has to carry and set up the easel and then bring out the chair and lastly the paints. I picked a corner of the garden where I can sit with my head in the shade and yet stretch my legs out in the sun. If I could, I would bake all the pain out of them.

Someone frequently comes out to check on me. I want to be annoyed by it, but I cannot—more often than not it is Reine, and more often than not I ask her to do something for me.

There is no clear thing in the garden to draw the eye at this angle but it does not matter—at least I am not inside painting another plate of fruit or vegetables. Though the lemon was not too bad. It is impossible to think dark thoughts with that much yellow.

WE HAVE THE FÊTE tomorrow and Marguerite Guillemet is here for a few days, willing to pose for me in each of her charming hats.

I have no trouble playing my part, and in some ways it brings its own comfort: I flatter, I cajole, I never speak what is on my mind.

Bellevue

I PAINTED ANOTHER LITTLE watercolor for La Lemonnier, complete with flags to honor the day, but when I finished the thing I felt piqued.

So instead of flirting with her, I told her I would not write to her again since she never responds. And sent it off before I could change my mind.

Vive l'amnestie.

THESE PAST DAYS I have been painting Marguerite Guillemet in the same corner of the garden I painted last week. Not because I like it so much but because I did not have the energy to search out another spot. In that spot I know exactly when I can sit with my legs stretched out in the sunlight, and for how long. This first painting is from a distance—she's a sketchy form in the greenery. But she is so willing to sit and so charming I plan to do another oil, closer up this time.

When I paint S or my mother in the garden, I cannot keep other thoughts at bay, but with Mlle Guillemet, I think only of the forms in front of me, the paint, and finding some witty, pleasant thing to say when she speaks to me. It is as if my thoughts are on their best behavior. I will myself to be cheerful, and I am cheerful. But when she leaves for the day I have to sleep immediately, and I barely have the energy to sit in the pony trap when the driver comes to take me to the clinic.

Mlle Guillemet wore a mauve coat but I made it blue. A better contrast with the red flowers.

AFRAID TO DOOM MYSELF as I write this, but for the past week—an entire week—my pain has decreased. Not just the number of spasms I have during the day and night, but the severity of each one when it comes. Not only has the intensity of the pain decreased a bit, but I somehow am better able to weather what I do feel. I know, I know—that only makes sense. It is easier to bear pain that involves less agony. But I mean something different.

I think I have gone about feeling my pain in the wrong way.

These past months, I have been waiting for the day that the pain stops, or at least becomes so negligible that it does not consume my thoughts or wake me from sleep. And those days have come. But when pain returns, I view it as a failure on my part, and I rail against what I feel. And that is another kind of failure. I steel myself against the next spasm, I will myself to endure, and it is all battle. I fear the next assault, I think of the pain as an army that overruns me, I am on guard against it always in public because I do not want to fall again and suffer that humiliation.

But I have not tried to live with my pain. I have not tried to think, upon waking, that I will weather the pain. I have not tried to think that, just as I once had to gain my sea legs onboard the *Havre*, I have to learn to walk steadily on my legs as they are now.

I suppose I did not want to admit that defeat, either. If I learn to live with my pain, it means I accept that I cannot be free from it. That my health, as I once knew it, is not a state to which I can return. Instead I have fought and fought.

I think my fear and my fighting have made things worse. But it is impossible not to want to fight when I have fought everything for so long—

I also seem to have a bit more movement in my left leg. It is infinitesimal, and at first I thought it was my imagination, but Materne sees it, too. A couple more degrees of flexing.

TODAY I WALKED OUT to the kitchen and found Mlle Piolet on her hands and knees scrubbing the floor, working her way back to the doorway. When she heard me, she sat back on her heels and turned a bit to look at me.

"You will have to wait a bit, m'sieur," she said, pushing hair out of her eyes with the back of one wrist. "I had something on my shoes and made a mess here."

"That's all right. I wanted a bite to eat is all."

"I can bring you something in a bit if you like."

"Don't trouble yourself, mademoiselle," I said, waving my hand and making as if to turn. And I did turn partway, but not before I saw her go back to scrubbing. For a moment I let myself watch her hips and ass move under her skirts, and then I forced myself to walk away with the beginning of an erection.

After months of impotence, I really did not know whether to laugh or shout. But I did neither. I closed the door and lay down on the bed, rubbed and pulled on myself, just like a schoolboy. I thought briefly of Reine Piolet, and then of Méry, but in the end it was enough to feel the thing myself, to feel my cock wet with its own happiness—

I will have to tell Materne about it. An erection as an indicator of health.

STILL NO WORD FROM Lemonnier. Even the newspapers described how prettily lit up her father's garden was for the fête, but she will not write about it to me.

I painted four pages of Mme Guillemet's skirts and shoes—little nothings that I planned to send to Lemonnier to amuse her—but I did not. I sent them today to La Dame Guillemet instead, and told her that I was feeling better and better.

Bellevue   23 JULY 1880

IN A LETTER FROM Méry today:

I have not washed a floor since I was fourteen. You must have a very potent imagination if you are able to have a fantasy about me scrubbing one.

Bark-laughed when I read it.

LÉON PACKAGED AND SENT off *Chez le Père Lathuille* to the salon in Ghent. Even though it got a little attention this spring, no one bought it. And no one can buy it if it is sitting in my studio.

I purposely chose it because it is a "lighter" work, but who knows? Maybe the Belgians will find the same faults with it that the Parisians did. But I hope someone will buy it. Materne and these water treatments are not cheap, and I need the money.

I PAINTED MY MOTHER reading in the garden. She made me promise not to show too much of her face. As if that were possible to do with her hat—

Silence still on the other front.

LA LEMONNIER HAS BEEN SICK. Some kind of serious fever. I did not hear it from her—Léon told me.

My callous relief that there was a real reason for her not writing and not just something directed at me.

When I began this notebook, this endeavor of writing about my life, I swore to myself there was a certain level of information I would not include—no information about my dalliances or affairs. I thought I should not add to my transgressions by writing about them in detail. And yet I write endlessly about my efforts to woo a woman young enough to be my daughter, about the lengths I go to in order to get a response.

In these pages I make abundantly clear the kind of man I am.

Bellevue   9 AUGUST 1880

TONIN HAS COME FOR a visit and it is both good to see him and painful. When he arrived yesterday and I went to greet him, I saw in his face just before he embraced me a confirmation of what I know to be true.

I am no better.

I fool myself sometimes if I have a particularly good day or a handful of them, and my arousal the week before ignited hope—I want to believe I am improving. But Tonin saw me from the distance of a couple of months and rated me with a true appraisal.

The sun helps, and fresh air. Adequate rest. All the time in the water seems to have helped me keep my range of movement. But better? Truly better? Even the few degrees extra I can flex my leg on good days are very little in the scheme of things. At best, one can say I have slowed my deterioration.

Tonin and I walked, and then there was no hiding it. My left leg still drags behind me. I still cannot bend it at the knee. So I told him I preferred to take the path down to the river, as it was easier for me than walking uphill. He did not take my arm but at certain spots he walked close enough to me that I could reach out to him if I needed him. All done without saying anything.

When we came upon a young girl selling flowers, I said, "See? There's the proof. If I were really any better, if I were really my old self, I would run back and grab my paint box so I could paint her portrait."

He looked at me with such a mixture of understanding and love and sadness I had to turn away from him. The last time I saw such a look on his face was at my father's funeral.

This is how I walk, even on a good day. My right leg takes a step. If I am fortunate, my left leg bears my weight while my right foot is midair. When my right foot comes back to the ground, my left leg can move forward, but because I cannot bend my knee, my movement comes mostly from my hip.

And what is my right leg doing when my left leg is attempting to swing its foot far enough above the ground so my foot does not scrape? It is tightening, holding me upright, straining with the effort. It is also waiting—waiting for my left leg to arrive.

That is the theme of my days, and what I should title this memoir: *Waiting for My Leg.*

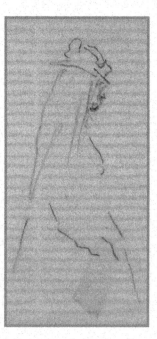

She told us she earned two francs a day for her flowers. I gave her three and so did Tonin—

"WHY NOT WRITE TO me about your erection? Flaubert wrote constantly about his, and about his 'self-flagellation.' He masturbated for the sake of art and made no secret of it. Why shouldn't you?"

    —Conversation with Tonin over a third glass of wine

TONIN LEFT YESTERDAY AND this morning I avoided my morn-
ing treatment. I went to the pool but did not go and see M. Victor afterward because I could not bear the idea of making small conversation or
sitting in that tiled room.

Mainly I did not want to be touched.

I asked the pool attendant to tell M. Victor I would not be in for my
massage, and he simply nodded. But of course this is not a prison, nor is it
a factory—no one came to reprimand me.

In this way I learned two things. My message was greeted so ordi-
narily that I suddenly knew people must beg off treatments with a certain
regularity, and whatever dramatic notion I had of myself in that moment
existed only in my mind and was not apparent to others. My petulance
was for me, and me alone. Though, to be clear, I never meant for M. Victor
to be the audience, nor Materne, nor S or my mother or Léon—

Sometimes, if such a mood comes over me, I go back over the litany.
The spring of *Olympia*. The trip to Spain, when I wanted to howl like a
dog and be left to lick my wounds. The show in 1867 that no one attended,
when my own mother had to plead with me to stop the "downward slide,"
as well she should have, since it was her fifty thousand I spent to mount it
and promote it. All the insults and silences. Every lie and subterfuge with
Léon. My own endless sins of omission and commission. I have no short-
age of black thoughts—I have had a surfeit for years. This illness and not
being able to walk normally are just the latest additions.

In the past when I had setbacks, I would throw my tantrums and rant
my rants, and I would often do it while I was out walking. I would walk
for hours, arguing in my mind, railing against everything. I walked until
my mind stopped, however long that took. An hour, two hours. Days. I
would walk until I was exhausted, until I was just a body. Then I would
look around for something to sketch or paint. I would boil the world

down to line and color, and that would be my broth. And I would begin again, I would begin to work again.

That is the worst part—I used to walk in order to lose myself. To forget myself. My legs were faithful companions, capable of carrying me from Batignolles to Gobelins and back home, but even that is wrong to say because I never thought about my legs. They were simply there, they were simply me, and they carried me. Now it takes all my thinking power simply to walk, and I have to think about my legs and feet and toes with every step. Yet I also know that no matter how much I do think, they will betray me again—I will fall again. It is inevitable. But how is it that one's own bones and nerves and muscles can become so disloyal?

My final black thought for the day? I know in my heart that one day I will look back on this day and wish it could come again. And I will think that because things have grown worse.

WHEN I ASKED, M. VICTOR told me people do sometimes miss hydropathy treatments. "But you are one of the most consistent, M'sieur Manet," he said then.

Good. I get a high mark for delusion.

I have not mentioned to him or Materne the most recent development, but I will write it here, in my "confessional": I am beginning to feel the same tingling sensations in my hands that I once felt in my feet, back before real pain began.

For days I feel nothing at all, feel absolutely normal, and then the sensation will come over me, like someone running a feather over my skin. Then tiny needling begins, and then a dense numbness sets in. If it happens to me while I am holding a pen or a brush, I can keep hold of the thing, but my fingers go dead. They turn to stone for a time—as heavy as stone and with as little sensation. Feeling only comes back bit by bit.

It happened the other day when I started a little watercolor. I watched the pigments drying and could not get the brush to move in the way I needed. The moisture dried before I could work it. I threw the page in the trash.

Bless me, Father Notebook. It has been thirty years—a lifetime— since my last confession.

I WANT LÉON TO send a couple of paintings off to that exhibition in Besançon, but I have to write to Tonin to ask for help first. If you do not know a deputy or a senator, it is pointless—you are like a pickpocket searching for a wallet.

M. Oudet is the senator there, but I am not sure if Tonin knows him or not.

STILL NO WORD FROM Isabel Lemonnier. I thought some kind of flow had started between us because of my little paintings, some kind of give-and-take. But she has better things to do than reply to me.

I have been tolerated only, not desired.

She does not know I had days when I could walk into a room and pick a woman—or better still, have her pick me.

Give me a willing partner, a woman who is unafraid of her appetite. They exist in all walks of life: demimondaines who came to my studio eager to meet me, and working-class girls I met in cafés and on the streets, like Victorine—but also society women who, away from their husbands and families, made their predilections known. I often did not know their life stories or philosophies and they did not know mine, and yet we gave each other pleasure, perhaps a greater pleasure than we might have felt free to take if we had been bound to see each other again in social circles or some prolonged affair.

Why do we only prize that which is long-lived? Obsession with the classical, with things which have lasted for a thousand years, poisons our thinking, convincing us that something only has value if it endures. A liaison that lasts only a night plays a role just as an affair that carries on over years does. One does not appreciate a moonflower less because it is not a linden tree.

In love as well as art I esteem the ephemeral. And if that is what has landed me here with Dr. Materne, then it is life itself that brought me!

TODAY IT DRIZZLED AND MISTED, so I only stood in the doorway looking out at the garden. I was just about to turn back to come inside
when some small, glinting bit caught my eye near a low wall. I thought I
saw black and yellow, and it puzzled me—was it a tube of paint?

So I went out into the moist air, walking slowly because I did not
want to slip in the wet grass, and as I got closer I saw what it was.

A salamander.

And before I could think, I leaned down and cupped my hands
around it and scooped. And stood up, my hands like a loose cage. When
I drew my thumbs back and peered inside, I saw the bright yellow spots
and moist black skin of its back, and then it turned itself around so I could
see its head. The black beads of its eyes. And then it climbed on top of my
index finger, out of the cage of my palms, and I kept moving my hands,
one over the other, so it would have a new place to climb onto. And this
went on for a little while, the salamander climbing over the terrain of my
hands again and again. Then, because I did not want it to fall and because
it so clearly wanted to be away from my imprisonment, I bent down again
and put the salamander back on the rock wall, and from there it scurried
quickly down into the grass. It moved with great purpose in its strange
way: right hind leg and right front leg, then left hind leg and left front leg.
I followed it for a moment and then stopped when I could no longer make
it out among the blades of tall grass.

After the salamander disappeared, I looked down at my hands,
expecting to see some trace of slippery slime, as a snail leaves—but there
was nothing. Just the fine bits of mist that were falling.

Only when I came back inside the back door did it hit me that I had
done exactly what I did when I was a boy, trapping toads and frogs in my
hands. That I had leaned over and stood back up, and then leaned over and
stood up again, and then walked through the yard and back to the house

without once thinking about my legs. That I had done it all without hesitation. Without consequence.

How is it even possible?

When Mlle Piolet came into the hallway to see if I needed anything, I must have looked strange because she said, "M'sieur, did something happen?"

I wanted to tell her, but I could not. Instead, I ran my hands over my face and beard and said, "It's damper than I thought." And kept the salamander to myself.

THE SALAMANDER HAS CHANGED my entire notion of things. I am still trying to fathom how I leaned over without thought or worry. And I suppose it is not entirely true that I made the movement just as if I were I boy—as a boy I would have squatted down. But still, I did bend down from the waist, and I know one knee flexed. I am sure of it.

But more than that, I cannot explain the change I feel in my concept of my body—as if it were my body again, and not a stranger, not a betrayer. This feeling has gone on for days now, and while I have not told Materne the reason for my change of attitude, he noted it in today's checkup.

"You are walking with greater confidence and fluidity," he told me.

Fluidity—I wanted to laugh. Wanted to tell Materne about the salamander's moist skin and how I rubbed my hands over my face when I came inside.

But the story would sound foolish or fantastic, so I kept silent. But it is all perfectly clear in my mind that the whole experience with the salamander unlocked something in me. Bending to catch it, catching it quickly, straightening to examine it in the loose cage of my hands—all of it done without thinking—it made me remember what it was like to move easily. My body remembered it.

Not just recent memories, either—memories from years ago, when I was a boy, unlocked from some place in my body. How else could I suddenly be back at Collège Rollin, doing gymnastics with all the other boys? How else could I be in the dimly lit room with its hanging ropes that we used to climb, and best of all, the wooden horse that I flew over like a champ? I once again felt what it was like to go over that wooden vault— legs out to a side, over and over. And, when I got up the nerve, going up over the thing in a handstand.

A handstand—a boy's dare. But I wanted to do it, so I ran at the horse. I had no idea exactly of how I would get my body up and over, but something in my body knew. So I ran at the thing. I ran at the thing with a picture in my mind of my legs going up above me, and I placed my hands on the wood, and that was the last thing I really knew—until my legs were up above me. And at some point in the handstand, when my legs were above me and just beginning to fall naturally and easily through the air, I felt a weightlessness. As if I were flying. And I understood that though I had touched the horse for a moment with my palms, what I had really done was fly. And then I was done, on the other side of the horse, upright, a feeling of weightlessness still inside me.

Bending to catch the salamander somehow conjured that day in the gym, and it was not a memory in my mind—it was a body memory.

I think too much about my legs, about falling, about pain. My mind has become too involved: I think about each step, I hesitate, I plan. And none of it helps. I do not walk any more surely and my pain does not decrease because I think.

But since the salamander—I can somehow shut off my mind. I can somehow allow my legs to do what they need to do. Because they know. And from time to time when I need to remind myself, when I want that feeling of weightlessness and sureness and knowing and not thinking to wash over me again, I rub my hands over my face and beard and up into my hair. I bathe in salamander mist.

THIS AFTERNOON WE HAD strange weather, going from heavy clouds to rain to a brief moment of hail. Tiny stones no bigger than peas, and almost immediately after the hail, the sun came out. Reine Piolet and I stepped out into the garden to pick up some of the melting bits before they disappeared entirely, and we crunched them in our teeth like candy. The whole thing made me remember the letter I sent to Baudelaire after *Olympia* got savaged: I told him the injuries and insults fell on me like hail. But today that comparison seemed absolutely wrong.

These hailstones did no damage in the garden. They glinted like small jewels on leaves, petals, and grass. We could hardly pick them up without melting them, and if we tried to hold them in our hands to look at them, they disappeared.

If only my injuries from that time had disappeared as quickly. Instead they stayed with me for years. What disappeared instead was me. I do not mean the trip to Spain when I removed myself from all of it, when I absented myself—I mean part of me ceased to exist. The spring inside me broke. I spent years trying to fix it.

When I think of the money I spent on that private exhibition in '67, I still want to die.

I thought if I could appeal to people directly, if I could get them to understand my vision—that every day when I walked down the street I would see scenes and people a thousand times more compelling and beautiful and worthy than romanticized myths. I wanted people to understand that their own fierce lives were more profound than anything from the past. I wanted people to see themselves.

But mainly I put on that show so I would not disappear entirely. And it was a waste.

The effort was wasted, and so was the money. And the money was not mine to waste. It was Eugénie's—it was my mother's money, for god's sake.

She tried to talk to me about the ruinous path I was on, but she should have done more. She should have disowned me that year and left me to fend for myself.

It is all so clear to me now—what I was trying to do, and why it was doomed. You cannot demand that people see what you see. When I think of all of it, I wonder why I kept on. I was thirty-three in 1865, the age of Christ when he died. I think I did die a little that year. And I think when I came back from Spain and went on painting it was partly because of Velázquez but also partly because I did not know what else to do.

I THINK I COULD only write what I wrote yesterday because of the salamander. It somehow gave me strength to look back in time. How can that possibly be? But it is true. When I remember those moments in the garden with that moist black and yellow form in the mist, I feel a sense of absolute peace. As if nothing could hurt me again. I think my gods are Velázquez and dragonflies and salamanders—

A VISIT FROM ÉMILIE Ambre today. We talked about music, how well seated this house is, how pleasant the summer has been, and about her upcoming tour—she leaves next month. Once we broached that subject, it was impossible not to acknowledge the failure she and Gaston de Beauplan experienced last year to get any significant attention for *The Execution of Maximilian* after dragging the thing along on last year's trip.

Not that I blame her for it—I hold Beauplan accountable for the dismal results of the "tour," if one can call two desultory showings in New York and Boston a tour. I believe he wanted to be seen to be having some role on that voyage other than just her lover, so he concocted the plan of promoting the painting as she sang in different cities. But he did not have the connections he needed to make a success of the thing, and it ended up being an expense.

I will say I had to marvel at how deftly Mlle Ambre handled the topic. She turned to me and said feelingly, "What a pity it did not result in a sale. But I am sure you are relieved to have your masterpiece home safely in your studio. I am still so honored that you entrusted us with it, but how you must have missed it!"

"It is I who was honored, mademoiselle," I told her, and then changed the subject. I did not want to admit that when the thing was delivered back to the studio, I had Léon check it for damage and then leave it in its crate. I did not have the heart to see it go back on the studio wall—

AFTER REINE PIOLET WASHED the breakfast dishes, she dried her hands on her apron and checked her hair with her fingers, searching for strands that had pulled loose from the roll.

Jeannot Piolet in a hat.

Bellevue

BECAUSE WE ARE STAYING here until the end of October, Méry
thought I was worse. Some of my letters this summer were so bleak I think
I must be partly to blame. I should tell her the story of the spotted salamander instead. She would understand the thing—she has a taste for the
esoteric. But I am not sure I want to tell anyone the story. It is mine, and
I feel protective of it.

I thought I could smell a bit of her perfume on the letter today, so I
keep pressing my nose to the paper. First the peonies, now this. One can
starve for fragrances, too.

Beau chevalier qui partez pour la guerre,
Qu'allez-vous fair
Si loin d'ici?
Voyez-vous pas que la nuit est profonde,
Et que le monde
N'est que souci?

Why do I keep repeating this old bit of Musset? What brought it to mind?

Baudelaire always said Musset as too melancholy, too dramatic, and I never disagreed. Yet I remember Musset's musical verses more easily than I do any of B's!

You who seek fame and reputation,
Your spirits, too, will be forgotten—

Bellevue

WROTE TO ANTOINE G. to ask him to call in a favor with Lockroy. I
sent a still life to Marseilles for them to consider, but without someone to
intercede, the thing will be overlooked.

I seem to be asking for favors a lot these days—like a beggar on the
street. And yet isn't that true of all of us? Most of us have but a few coins
to rub together in this life.

VICTORINE GREETS ME FROM the center of the longest of the walls, while Méry in her black stockings hangs in the middle of the south wall. Yet even their vivid presences cannot bring this space to life. Even with canvases hung one above the other, the place seems empty—and I do not mean just the huge gap from *Execution of Maximilian*. The place is cavernous. There is simply not enough to fill it. There is not enough of me.

Can it be that I miss the close confines of my "chamber" in Bellevue? The garden I dismissed as sad when I first arrived? But I do miss them, along with the closeness of the trees, the incessant cawing of crows, and the sound of Reine Piolet's footsteps, so much brisker than my mother's, so much louder than S's.

The truth is I have simply not spent enough time in this new studio for it to feel like mine.

So I am coming here. I am attempting to inhabit it as much as possible. And while it is a great relief to be away from the monitoring I could not escape in Bellevue, I am afraid there is not enough of me to fill this new space. Even now I am not out in the big room but in the small side room. It is the only spot that has any intimacy to it, so here I stick like a barnacle.

Which surprises me. I thought I would want nothing so much as to go to La Nouvelle Athènes as soon as I returned. And I did go to La Nouvelle Athènes—once. It is not the distance—I am walking more steadily than I have in months. But I have no desire to reenter the conversation about what I make of so-and-so, or to try to top the last clever remark, or answer any questions about what I am working on. So when I ventured out the other day, I went to a small place on rue Tarbé, a place I never have been to that was mostly filled with workers, and where I saw no one I knew. I sat at a table, my bad leg stretched out, and I ordered a beer. It was the thing I wanted, and it was the thing I let myself do: to pretend for just an hour that it was another life I was leading. I wanted to occupy a spot other than my own.

When people ask me how I am, I do not know how to account for these last six months. I cannot be honest and say that I have been living with pain as if it were my lover, that this lover abused me so greatly that at times I cried, that I only learned how to weather her caresses in the last month, and that it took a visit from a salamander in the garden one day to teach me how to live with her as peaceably as I can. I would sound like a madman. I do sound like a madman, even to myself.

So instead I must lift my chin and reply, "I am doing well enough." And then whoever it is that is inquiring is comforted that they did their duty in asking, and can go away peacefully because I have not insisted on telling the truth.

And it is not that I have not reentered things here: Bracquemond and I will pay a visit to Goncourt next week, and I am to see Rochefort soon—Desboutin said he can arrange it. Rochefort's escape has me thinking of the sea, of the *Kearsarge*, of green waves, dolphins, and flying fish. Méry has promised to come and sit for me—to come as many times as I want her.

But right now it all feels distant. Only in this little room off the big studio can I be myself. Only here has any real work begun.

I had Léon hang paper directly on all the walls, waist-high and three feet tall so I can work on things while I sit. I am drawing dragonflies, one after another after another. I want to get a feeling for what it means to create something of that size, something that surrounds the viewer on all sides.

I have started on one wall, covering it with varying sizes of dragonflies, all in pastel. It is the quickest thing, and I can play at the color of the sky. I work on it and then I pull the chair back and sit, staring. Sometimes I can almost believe I am there along the river again, in that glowing blue light, with all those wings above me.

Léon is the only one who knows. I am going to have him to drag the chaise longue in here this weekend—I want to be able to sleep in here when I get tired, among the glinting dragons.

MY SHOCK TODAY WHEN Léon unpacked *The Execution of Maximilian* and got it back onto the wall for me.

It sounds ridiculous—it is my painting, and I have lived with it constantly since '68. But when Émilie Ambre took it away and I went to Bellevue, I got a break from it. I do not claim that I forgot it—but its particulars, as well the grandiose whole of it, became a bit distant, and today I somehow saw it with fresh eyes.

First there is the epic size of the thing. If you stand in front of it, you are forced to reckon with the firing squad as well as those about to be executed. All are the same size as you—they are your equals. You have to looks at the faces of Mejía, Miramón, and Maximilian, but the cadre of soldiers remains anonymous—you must peer over the shoulders to see the exact moment Mejía is struck by bullets, to see Maximilian and Miramón grasping hands as they wait to die. The only soldier whose face you do see is the sergeant, who calmly readies his gun, so that after his men kill Miramón, he can in turn fire upon Maximilian, who is already a pale ghost. The onlookers behind the wall form some kind of Greek chorus, or gaze like powerless cherubim at the spectacle of death below.

Seeing the painting today, I wondered not only how I had the energy to paint it time after time, reworking composition after composition as news of the murderous day made its way back to France, but also how I survived the political aftermath. I could not have created an image more critical of Louis Napoleon, or more incendiary, unless I depicted Maximilian with the face of a sacrificial lamb. Where others murmured their dissent and concern, I shouted. I boldly painted my protest—and my own destiny—life-size.

Even though very few people saw the painting in any one of its versions, word "got around." The only real mystery to any of this is how I ever again had anything accepted by the state-sponsored mouthpiece of the Salon. I both denounced and wanted recognition from the same entity.

Which is proof of a kind of madness or hubris.

But it all seems very clear now that I was rejected as much for my moral choices as for my use of color and line. It is strangely freeing to realize—

IF I WAS IN any doubt about what I missed this fall, Goncourt filled in all the blanks for me. He is still riding high from the publication of his book this year—and absolutely willing to hold forth about the ever-widening scope of his success and talent.

"I create with words the shades and nuances an artist renders with his brushes," he told me. "Nothing is too subtle, nothing too exotic, for me to do it justice on a page."

He is insufferable. And yet, and yet—

Tonight he went on and on about some women's dresses that the Japanese artist Utamaro painted, decorated with starfish. About sashes painted the color of goldenrod and moss. His love of it all was infectious, intoxicating. I wanted to see the paintings he described, wanted to feel the things he felt.

His pompousness is bearable because he loves everything so *hard*.

EACH MORNING I RUN my hands over my face, up into my hair, and down over my beard. I cross my arms over my chest and run my hands over my arms and belly, then down over my haunches, my knees, my shins. I think of the salamander and the misty day, I think of flying through the air at Collège Rollin. I say—not just in my mind but out into the air—I say, "I trust my legs."

I trust my legs.

I trust my legs.

I trust my legs.

GONCOURT MUST HAVE GOTTEN under my skin after all, because today I went to Sichel's. In the rich chaos I found one piece I could not leave behind. Not a woodblock print at all but a tiny wood netsuke.

A woman bathes in a tub. One foot in the water, the other foot up on the rim of the tub, where she bends to soap it.

A small frog also perches on the rim of the tub. He sits behind the woman and looks up. At her *chose*.

I could not stop looking at the figure once I picked it up. In truth I looked more at the frog than anything.

It is catch as catch can at Sichel's, and as I went up to the counter to pay for the thing, Ephrussi approached me. So caught up in the netsuke, I had not seen him there among the displays of wares, sleekly dressed as he always is, his beard so smooth it looks like a pelt. After expressing pleasantries and delight about seeing me, he said, "Now the real question. What are you buying?"

When I showed him the netsuke, he took it from my hand and let it lie in his palm. He stood looking down at it for a long time, not saying anything. Then brought it up to his eye.

"The frog," he said, shaking his head.

It made me smile.

We made plans then for him to come by the studio, and I told him to give my regards to his neighbor, Mlle Lemaire.

"She adores your portrait of her, you know."

"I adore her," I told him.

Only then did he give back the netsuke.

What is it about the smallness of such things? Do they remind us of trinkets we had as children? Is it that you see them as much with your fingertips as you do with your eyes? Yet small paintings also have a charm that larger works cannot.

I think some of it is that you have to get close to see. You come in as if for a kiss, so there is that nearness. The intimacy is built in—first by the artist, who had to do close work to make the piece, and then by the viewer, who must finish the embrace.

The nude with her messy hair and small breasts charms, but the real action is in the frog—

THE WEEK OF EPHRUSSI.

He came just as he said he would. Walked the studio as he always does. When he asked to see what I had been working on since he saw me last, I had to pull things out from where Léon had everything stacked. Pastels, watercolors, oils—I let him see the lot.

He is a curious looker—he takes his time. He says gracious things, to be sure, but mostly he does not talk. He is comfortable looking in silence. This spring when I met him, that seemed strange—the writer of all those *Gazette* articles having nothing to say—but I understand now. He looks, he feels, he thinks—and only afterward does he express his ideas. There is no torrent of words from him, no stream of observations. You could not find a person more different from Goncourt, I think—and yet they are both champions of art and devoted to articulating their passions on the page.

Of everything I showed, he picked the most unlikely. Or maybe it was not unlikely at all. It is like no other of the works, and he saw that immediately.

The bunch of asparagus. White stalks with mauve-purple tips, piled on some greens that Reine brought from the garden when I asked. Creams and greens and grays to go with that pinkish purple. I thought there was something so delicate in the coloring, like the nacre inside a shell, or the pink shadows beneath an eye.

"Perfect in its homeliness," Ephrussi said, taking the thing up with his fingertips, holding it in front of him. "Who wants a peach or a pomegranate when one can have this awkwardness?"

We agreed on 800 fr., and he was so adamant I wrapped it in a clean cloth so he could take it with him.

"I don't think I can let it go to be framed," he said.

It only takes an interaction like that to unman me. If people knew the effect of their words—

The first day I met Méry, she said a simple, kind thing about my *Laundry* painting and I nearly wept. How my critics would laugh if they knew the power a bit of praise had over me. The ugly things I have learned to steel myself against but not the generous ones.

Which is as it should be. In this dog of a life one has to endure.

EPHRUSSI SENT PAYMENT—1,000 fr., not the 800 fr. we agreed upon. If it were anyone else I would wonder what point was being made. Somehow I do not mind it coming from him. He sees, he understands, he champions. A patron. I do not have much experience with the phenomenon—

Yes, of course he sent the money because he could. But I genuinely think he sent it because it pleased him to do so.

What would life have been like if the path had been just a bit easier? How many years did I lose to doubt? Something broke in me altogether in 1865, I know.

I appreciate the sympathy as much as the money. I need to do something for him in return.

MÉRY COMES TOMORROW. IN her note she said she would be wearing a new hat that makes her look like a Russian princess.

Working on Ephrussi's gift—

YOU HAVE A MOUTH and fingers—

That is what Méry said when I could not "stand to." After all that I wrote to her this summer about my glorious erection, yesterday there was nothing. I felt a bit of pressure in my groin, that is all. That was when she said it—*you have a mouth and fingers.*

And moved my hand to her sex.

AFTER WEEKS OF FEELING STRONG, for the past two days only lethargy and piercing needles in my feet—as if I were a specimen mounted on a board.

The pain is real enough, but I think the fatigue is partly mental. The episode with Méry has depressed me, though, if I am honest, I have had such difficulties for years, starting back in '70. At the time I thought my inability to perform was a result of poor food, illness, and worry—everyone suffered the winter of the siege. But now I believe that was the real start of my decline. I had pain in my feet then, too, and weakness in my ankle, and for weeks I had boils on my ass from being in a saddle hour after hour—

But what difference does it make how or when it began? This aspect of the disease is here now, and it seems the erection I experienced this summer was a stroke of luck, not a sign of recovery. I suppose I should be grateful that all of it happened with Méry. If I had been impotent with that prudish young woman La Lemonnier, what a scene she would have caused.

I need to shake this lowness. I need to go back to the way I felt the day of the salamander.

MÉRY'S CUNT TASTES LIKE pears and salt.

Méry
The rainy day I saw the salamander
The salamander
Hydropathy (not cold showers but the swimming peacefully, up
    and down the pool)
Dew on peonies
The sound of Reine Piolet washing dishes
Netsuke of the woman bathing
Skin of the frog watching the woman bathing
The moistness of them all—

SENT OFF MY GIFT to Ephrussi—a single stalk of asparagus on the edge of a table, as if it had fallen from the bigger bunch. Mauve, purple, olive, cream, goldenrod, and gray.

"Your bunch is missing one," I put in the note.

ROCHEFORT. STRONG ROCK!

I saw him yesterday, briefly, and he was, by turns, stoic and imperious. Ever the marquis, no matter his politics. But more importantly, one gets the impression of someone who is not at rest. I kept sensing that he viewed our meeting as a great favor he was granting me. Perhaps it is the magnificent shock of graying hair rising up from his head that gives him such an air of impatience. It makes him look as if he is caught in mid-stride, hurrying off to some action—

But the story, that is another thing. I knew I was hearing something well rehearsed, but it was impossible not to be moved by hearing him say, "We set out after nightfall, six men in a whaleboat."

I am still turning over in my mind the details, but this one sticks with me: when they escaped the harbor in Nouméa in New Caledonia, they had to row out to an Australian ship called, of all things, *Peace, Comfort and Ease*, commanded by a Captain Law, no less. One cannot make up these things—the stories life hands us are more fantastic than any novel.

I want to talk it over with Mallarmé and see what he makes of it. But I know for certain that I need to see a whaleboat. I want to see the form of the vessel that carried them across the water.

Paris 5 DECEMBER 1880

IN TALKING ABOUT SOME day on the voyage home, Rochefort said, "The sea—no wonder the Arabs call it 'La Bleue.' There were days when it was molten cobalt."

I loved the look on his face when he said "La Bleue." As if it were a prayer!

I WALKED THE WAY I always do: right out of the building, up Saint-Pétersbourg, right onto the Boule. Everything was fine, I was looking ahead as I always do to the golden façade of the building across the Place—and that is when the vise gripped. A band of metal tightening across my left foot with such viciousness I gasped and stumbled. If I had not been so close to the wall of a building, if I had not had that to grasp at, I would have gone down entirely, as I did last year.

A waiter on Batignolles saw me—came up and offered to walk me to a table. I wanted to send him away, but instead I said, "If you would."

I sat in his restaurant until the vise grip eased. Until the sweat dried on my forehead. Even though it is December and the air so brisk it makes you wince, I was sweating as if I had run a race. Perhaps I should have gone home then, but I came here instead. I did not want the inevitable questions. *Don't you think, are you sure you should—*

If that waiter had been young, would I have accepted the help? The vain part of me says no. When I see Aristide working, even when it is me he is helping, I get so exasperated. You never think of health until it begins to fade. But the waiter today was almost my age, graying at the temples, and it was somehow easier to accept his aid. Yet even he had the advantage. He went on working his tables, nimble and surefooted, while I sat and sat.

TONIN CAME AND I told him about Rochefort.

"If I am to paint that escape, I need a whaleboat," I told him. "They were hugger-mugger in there, and I need to be able to see the dimensions. But where in Paris am I to get a whaleboat? A whaleboat!"

That's when he said—nonchalantly—that he might "know someone."

"That's not really your world, is it, old man?" I said.

"You don't know what circles I move in. Leave it to me."

For some reason it made me laugh. And yet it is true. Even when you know someone all your life, they can surprise you. S taught a man who, when he retired from his job at a bank, bought a piano and began to take lessons. He made his wife crazy because he had to start plinking away at scales like any schoolboy, but he wanted to learn. *And now I have the means and the time*, he told S.

Age is so misleading—you are the same on the inside as ever, only your outsides are different. Or, perhaps you have changed, but it is not like the younger self goes away—you just go on adding layers to the onion.

After Tonin left I thought about the whole incident in the street and how I envied even the middle-aged waiter at the café, and then I realized: just as I will one day miss my current state of health, one day I will look back and envy *exactly who I am today*. It is true already. When I think of the early days of this illness, when my left foot would tingle and begin to ache, or else go numb altogether, it upset and bothered me—and now I would give anything if those were my only complaints.

I could have told Tonin what happened the other day on the boulevard, and he would have understood. But I chose not to. To play the game a little longer, to keep the illusion going, even with a dear friend—is it asking so much?

MÉRY STOPPED BY TODAY in another new hat, a grand black affair with a plume. Her eyes pierced me with their blueness and their kindness, and I could not stop thinking of how she spared me that day. By insisting on her pleasure, she gave me something else to focus upon. But when I said that to her this afternoon, she just laughed.

"Women must always rejoice in men's pleasure," she told me. "Now you know what it means to be one of us."

I SENT A NOTE off to Rochefort and told him to pick a couple of days in January that would suit him. I need to get some things on the calendar so the winter does not yawn before me.

He told me he would sit for a portrait, but he said it grudgingly, so I wonder. He wants everyone to come to him, I believe.

I have no doubt any number of people will rush to pay homage in the way he demands. But some may court him for their own reasons, and he will not notice their ends because their tributes please him. They will form a mutual admiration society until it no longer serves their purposes.

A WEEK BEFORE CHRISTMAS and the only thing I want is for the whaleboat to arrive. Why does no one tell you that work, not love, is the real salvation?

Because if we told young people how life really was, they would beat us with their fists and ask why we brought them into this world.

YESTERDAY AFTERNOON I PICKED out a present for Berthe—a new easel that is supposed to be good for pastels—and wanted to have it delivered. But after I paid and said I wanted it sent to Mlle Morisot, my mind went blank. I could not remember her address, even though she has lived in that apartment for years, first with her mother and now with Eugéne. I could not for the life of me pull the detail from my memory.

One faulty moment, one forgotten fact. But it somehow became more. As I stood, trying to think of the street name and house number, I felt my mind empty entirely. Then a wave of dizziness came. The room spun off to the right and then came back to center, then spun off to the right again, over and over. I tried to look at the clerk, but I could not focus on his face. I wanted to say something to explain, but I could not think of the words to describe what was happening in my head. Could only stand there like an idiot, gripping the counter, waiting for the room to stop reeling. Even describing it now is making the sensation return—

When some moments passed, the clerk told me, *If Monsieur would like to return with the address.*

All that was left for me to do was nod. But the trial still was not over—I still had to make it out of the shop and onto the street. I did so by putting my hand onto one surface after another, the length of the counter, a table where they had pastels displayed, the doorframe, and on the building itself.

Outside, how long did I stand with my back against the façade? Away from the shop window so the clerk would not see? Five minutes? Twenty? And when the worst of the reeling passed, I got a carriage and had it bring me here.

How I did any of it without falling—

I felt stupid enough in the moment. But now all I can think about is that blankness, every detail in my mind gone and nothing to latch on to, and the dizzying vertigo that followed, for that is the word for what I experienced, I think.

First my impotence with Méry, and now this. What new symptom will present itself next?

I need to lie down. Need to lie on the chaise [*two illegible words*]—

TODAY THE ADDRESS CAME clearly to me without me even trying: Berthe lives on rue Guichard.

I do not want to remember any of it, and yet I want to put it down. I want to tell the truth about yesterday's fugue. About everything.

Whatever respite I experienced this autumn in Bellevue is over. Sometimes I feel as if someone were slicing open the front of my thigh, and other times this butcher peels the skin from my heel like an onion. The salamander's benediction has ended, no matter how often I pray to him and wash my face with water.

Yesterday, because I wanted to buy Berthe's gift, I spent the morning thinking of her. I have trained myself not to dwell on thoughts of her, and because I am so successful at it, I believed no harm would come to me from a few stray reminiscences. But the racing feeling in my mind began when I let myself remember the old agony of that affair. How fitting it was that I felt dizzy and blinded by that fit in the store—I was willfully blind in my behavior with her.

Or maybe what happened to me had no relation at all to thoughts or emotion. Sireday has always said the disease picks the brain or the body. If it picks the brain, as it did with my father and Gustave, there is a stroke or paralysis. Loss of speech and mental ability. If it picks the body, it begins in the legs, as it has with me. But what if there is a third route? A gradual weakening of both the mind and body? What then?

Now I want wooden whaleboats and sea waves, Rochefort's pock-marked skin—even Pertuiset's portrait with his new gun, which he has told me about at length: a double-barreled Devisme engraved with ivy leaves. Those are the things I have in front of me, so that is what I must choose to want. No lank black curls, no dark eyes obscured by a fan. No love, except that which is rooted in friendship, as it is between Méry and me.

Only work, and pleasure as I can find it. And the goddamned truth— I will tell it all to Sireday in the new year.

THE WHALEBOAT MEASURES twenty-seven feet long with a beam of a little more than five feet. The tiller and rudder are gone, as is the centerboard and tholepins. A shell of a boat. But that shell is sound, and some of the old gray paint still clings to the boards. From Le Havre to Paris, then here to the courtyard of the studio by cart—it is the last voyage this flaking old sea wolf will make.

It must have been a thing to see it ply the waters so close to the animals that dwarfed it. When I imagine the scene, it takes all my powers to incorporate the hundreds of details that must have bombarded the sailors. When I picture seeing the whale itself—the skin of its back or its blowhole or, most terrifyingly, its tail coming above the water—I feel transported back to the *Havre et Guadeloupe*, back to the water.

I cannot stay away from the thing. Cannot stop going out to the courtyard to stand or sit beside it, even though the weather has turned and I feel the bite of the cold in no time at all.

Would it all be so fresh in my mind if I had not just looked at the letters Léon brought? Perhaps. Perhaps the power of the whaler would have been so great that I would immediately be cast back to that time. And yet how much easier it is this way! To pick up thinking of the sea where I left off this summer—the pump was primed.

Yet so often it goes that way. I notice something, or find myself thinking of something, and I follow it in my thoughts and on paper. I sketch it and dwell on it and follow my obsession, only to find that it leads me somewhere, or that it gives me just such information as I need, or somehow informs the next painting. It may happen days or weeks later, or it may take months or even years. But that obsession becomes the focus of a painting, or a detail of a painting. Or else it may only come out in the mood of the painting and its expression. But when I need it, there is the thing in my mind, half or fully formed.

We all talk about "keeping our hand in," but it is more than that. You sketch because it ignites something in the mind. You stick with a thing because it gives your mind pleasure to stick with it. In the summer it was peonies and dragonflies and the hands of Reine Piolet, and this fall it was the salamander. Now it is this whaleboat.

Even with Tonin's help, it was not a thing that fell into my lap—I had to work to find it. Had to work for my obsession. But it does not matter. I would gladly pay more to have such a love as this old whaleboat with its double bows and peeling paint. Even in this skeletal form and missing all its gear I can feel its power.

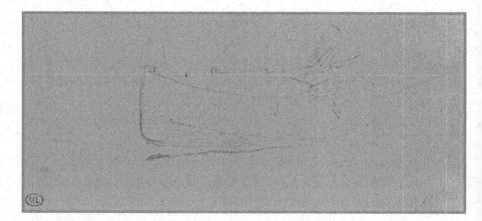

Paris   5 JANUARY 1881

BERTHE SENT A NOTE to thank me for the easel and along with it, a tiny, folded locket made of paper, painted yellow to look like gold. When you open the locket, on the left is a painted lock of hair. On the right, a little portrait of her.

As if she were not burned indelibly in my mind's eye—

ANOTHER THING NO ONE tells you about when you are younger: that in aging, one falls in love more easily. Not with people—that is as tricky as ever. I mean fall in love with things. The other day I wanted to weep when I saw the leafless trees along Batignolles, reaching upward with their limbs in the cold. Or the day I bought that easel, before everything began to swim, I passed by a display of gloves in a window and felt what I can only describe as an aching kind of love when I saw a pair made from emerald-green leather.

It is something women understand much sooner than men, I think. S has known it for some time. This summer when I was dithering over La Lemonnier's letters, she went about falling in love with her black kitten, who burrowed in her hair and learned to ride on her shoulders, who sleeps behind the crook of her knees every night. And in the end, who was smarter? The one who chased a pretty, callow face, or the one who has her love returned in spades each day by a spirit as passionate as any?

I can think such things in the presence of the whaleboat. It has known its share of desperate men. It does not judge but sits instead in silence.

WHAT NEWS COULD THERE BE? I knew. I knew without him telling me.

Reduced patellar response—nerves in my legs no longer work. My gait is more "ataxic," meaning I am more and more unstable. Worse than last year at this time, which I knew in my body but which he has some way of quantifying. When I told him about my impotence, he said that was often one of the first symptoms, and that I had a "longer run than most."

I wonder what my face looked like just then.

Without telling any of the details of the salamander, I asked him why I had been spared some of the worst in late summer and fall.

"Tabes is mysterious in its ways. Sometimes a remission occurs and lasts for a time."

"So it wasn't the effect of the water cure?"

"Perhaps. Perhaps not. It may have been a result of rest as much as anything else."

I laughed then. Actually laughed. All those hours in the pool, or being pummeled by M. Victor, or enduring the cold-water showers—for nothing!

"So I might have experienced the same remission if I took to my bed for a month," I said.

"You might have," Sireday replied.

On that point at least we agreed: spending time at Materne's clinic would likely be "useless." So that is one expense that may be avoided this summer.

"Édouard, there are medications for pain. Chloral, bromide. Morphine—"

But I am not yet at that point. I would rather go on making useless prayers to the salamander god. And drinking wine as palliative. I know the time for drugs will come. At the end, I was the one who gave my father morphine, often more than prescribed—my mother did not have the stomach for the injections. But they were the only thing to ease the agony we saw in his face. So I know about drugs. I do know.

A good, long run. Christ. But doctors can say anything. You pay them to lecture you, to insult you. I suppose he thought it was all part of telling the truth.

TWO MORE THINGS I learned from Sireday:

"Tabetics" experience a tightening in the chest and belly—he called it the girdle effect. So now I can picture that, a corset choking me.

"Formication" is the term for the feeling of insects crawling in and on your skin.

I plan to stick with pins and needles to describe my sensations. I see no need to bring lice or flies into it.

Jesus, what a sentence to write—

AT SOME POINT IN the night I woke up and felt an odd heaviness in my leg. For a moment I thought it was some kind of new manifestation of things—

It was Jicky.

For whatever reason, he had come to sleep with me and was lying partway on my calf. So I must not have been thrashing around too much. I would like to think he came because he somehow knew I was troubled, but I doubt it. At least I can say that about my leg: it still gives off heat.

That small, friendly weight against me—

Paris

I AM CLINGING TO this painting of Rochefort's escape as if to life itself. If for nothing else, I thank him for saving me from my thoughts.

The simple lines of the thing are eloquent the way only plain and workaday things can be. That left side of the boat is like a scythe, a scythe through the sea.

ROCHEFORT ON THE TILLER, the other men merely darkened figures—I am painting the story as he told it. Only his face is visible, lit by the phosphorescent sea giving off its own light. It must have been phosphorescent because Rochefort kept using the words "shining" and "glistening" for the sea, even though they departed at night. Had I not seen that glowing phenomenon for myself aboard the *Havre*, I would have been at a loss to render that golden zigzag behind the whaleboat, or the froth of golden wavelets hugging its port side.

We are all always the heroes of our stories, or the villains—we never play a bit part. I understand that. And yet there was something bigger than even Rochefort in his story, which was the sea itself. Teal troughs, aqua arcs, white tips of waves. It was joy to paint them. Those colors, the depths beneath them, and the whaleboat itself, all lit by an early dawn light.

To hell with the fact that they departed at night! To paint the thing, I needed color and light. At a certain point, truth must give way to the illusion of truth.

RAINING SO BADLY I cannot go out to sit beside the boat. Perhaps just as well—I need to begin on the portrait Pertuiset commissioned and for which he has already made partial payment. He wants some record of his younger days and has even loaned me a carte de visite from more than a decade ago. *Something along these lines*, he told me, but I know what he means: he does not want a current portrait of his aging self but an homage, a record of who he once was.

The whole request strikes me as indulgent. Comical even. Yet all I need do is think back to the summer and the prattle I wrote to La Lemonnier and I dare not lift a finger in accusation—we want to preserve our youth at any cost. This painting of Pertuiset will be like an insect in amber.

But I will do the thing exactly as he asks. He has always supported me—and I need the scratch.

Ah well. I hope the rain reminds the boat of the sea.

SO MILD TONIGHT THAT we all went into the courtyard—Toché, and Duret and his friend Deudon. We smoked and admired the whale-boat, at least what we could see in the light shining from the studio windows. Talk turned to voyages, and Toché asked if I ever was sorry I did not go to sea.

"I go to the sea all the time," I told him, smiling.

"I mean as a sailor. An officer."

"No, I tried it when I was young, and I am not sorry I let that profession go. Many days were dull," I said. "And the times we could not make land made me despair."

"Where was that?"

"Madeira and Tenerife. The weather was not in our favor. I was two months out of Le Havre before I walked on land again."

"I don't know if I could have stood it," Duret said. "Still, it must have been an adventure."

"Some parts more than others," I told him. "But yes, I caught a shark and ate porpoise and crossed the equator."

"And saw Rio," Toché said. "And thought of going to America."

"So you remember all those stories I told you, do you?" I asked. "No, I never really wanted to go to America. I just wanted to come back to Paris."

"How old were you then?" the fellow named Deudon asked.

"Seventeen."

"I was a schoolboy at seventeen," he told me. "I envy you."

Why is it sometimes good to stand out in the night, talking in dark like that? It feels out of the ordinary somehow. I could see Toché felt the same way—his eyes were glowing, and he looked impish, the way he does when he is pleased. After the talk of the sea, I was glad to let all of them do most of the storytelling, though. I liked standing back and watching their faces in half shadow.

After they left, I went back to the doorway and looked out at the whaleboat. How quiet the courtyard seemed after hearing those warm voices echo off the stones.

I AM FORTY-NINE TODAY. No celebration but no mourning, either. The sale of Duranty's things is next week, and it puts it all into perspective.

At his death, he was younger than I am now.

They say the infection that killed him was grotesque. You hope the thing you always hope—that he did not suffer—but you know he did. It is impossible not to suffer with that kind of foul thing.

That ridiculous duel we fought seems a lifetime ago, but it was not. It was just over a decade ago. The idea that I would threaten someone over words on a page seems utterly foreign to me now, but I did it. I stormed into the Guerbois and slapped him, actually slapped him. Hard enough to make my palm sting. I was incensed not so much over the words themselves but over the dismissiveness of the gesture: A "friend" writes a review of your work and instead of an actual review, jots down one sarcastic sentence. One insult.

It wounded me.

But of course a man cannot say that to another man—you cannot say to another man, *You hurt me.* So I slapped his face instead. And when we dueled, I sliced open the skin on his chest. Zola said when our swords clashed that first time, both blades wavered in the air from the impact. That is how headstrong we were, how convinced we were that we had been injured.

Now he is dead and I am a stumbling wreck. It's rich, rich. And so, Duranty, lame as I am, I will fight on for the both of us.

STARTING A SECOND PAINTING of Rochefort's escape. This time I want him to be unrecognizable, only a man among men on a boat on La Bleue, rowing for life. The sea will be the heroine this time with no competition from the hero, or at least a man who fancies himself a hero. The men will look like puppets in the boat this time—the water will be the star.

Why do I feel such antagonism toward Strong Rock? Maybe my feelings are just a reflection of his disdain for me.

Someone is stabbing my heel right now. It makes my foot shoot out from beneath me. I dance a jig. But I will paint this water-drama sitting down if I have to.

THIS MORNING IN BED—I want to write it down.

I was not awake yet but waking—I thought a round of spasms was starting. Prickles and needles in my legs. Then the image came: an octopus, iridescent red, pressed its body over my left hip and ass cheek, and wrapped its tentacles down my leg. I could see the moisture on its skin, the sleek, oval head, the bulbous eyes moving toward my cock—

I thought I was in for it then but nothing happened. I mean, yes, the needling and pricking continued, but nothing more. And the image dissipated as I woke.

A mottled red octopus. Straight from a Japanese woodblock.

Is it because of the whaleboat? All the thinking about the sea?

The red of the skin pulsed with life, the tentacles wrapped me in a tight embrace. In another moment my genitals would have been consumed—

This undated entry is on a small, separate sheet of paper and not part of the notebook proper. However, this was its location within the bound book, and judging by the indentations on the bound pages, it has been there always. —A. Sosset

NANA OPENED LAST NIGHT, and I had dinner with the Nittises, who wrote to me to say I might have a seat in their box if I wanted to go.

After we dined, just as we were about to eat dessert, Degas showed up. As executor, he presided over the sale of Duranty's effects, and he seemed keen to share his news of the dismal event.

"Things went for a good sum, mind you," he said.

As he shoveled roast beef into his mouth (his appetite unaffected by his role), he turned to Nittis and said, "Even your pastel fetched a couple hundred."

Nittis blanched—that is the only word for it—and then turned red. Two hundred francs is nothing to sniff at, but Degas had already informed us of other prices, so it was clear the sketch by Nittis fell a bit short. Yet even that unspoken conclusion was not enough for Degas.

"I suppose it is lucky so many of my friends were in attendance. They bid as much to buoy me up as anything."

That is the thing about Degas: everything is always about *him*.

Zola's play was fine—good, even—but I left after the third tableau. My foot was in a vise grip and I thought I would start to shout if I had to stay upright any longer.

I BOUGHT A STUPID concoction a couple of months ago—red jelly capsules in a six-sided amethyst bottle. I think I bought it as much for its prettiness as for its promises. I took a few and then stopped. Of course they were useless, and today I threw out the remaining capsules. Kept the little bottle.

It was the one thing I did not tell Sireday. I think I wanted to avoid the kind of lecture he gave me when I tried a remedy from Eugène's homeopath.

But if a remission from tabes came once for no reason, isn't it possible it can come again?

A WHITE HORSE HITCHED to a cart along Batignolles this morning kept turning his head, as if to see that his red and white plaid bag was
there. When I passed him, he bobbed his head a couple of times as if in
greeting. I nodded back at him.

The Infinite Patience of the Parisian Cart Horse, an exhibit by É.
Manet. No—all the stations of the cross, rendered with horses and carts
and carriages. I will call it The Lamentation of the Cart Horse.

THE LION IS A photographer's prop.

The trees are such as we have in France and nothing at all to do with Africa.

But Pertuiset loves this portrait I am making of him. When he comes to check on it, he smiles and says, "Not too shabby." I do not know if he is passing judgment on my painting or the self he sees depicted. What is certain is that I faithfully show his double-barreled gun and leather hunting boots, as well as his feathered cap that would have been stifling in African heat.

Perhaps the Salon jury will approve of this gun. It is not being fired at Maximillian or Mejía, nor are French soldiers using it on Communards at the barricades. And yet it is all the same story: the one with the gun wins, and those that lose are left in bloody heaps on the ground.

But the allegory will be lost on everyone. People think Pertuiset is a fool and a blunderer, and I agree—but but at least he is honest about the beasts he hunts, and more honest than Rochefort could ever be about anything. And if *Portrait of M. Pertuiset, Lion Hunter*, gives me the opportunity to create a narrative about power and butchery that makes it past the censors, then I will be the one beholden to Pertuiset.

All the same, I am putting something unexpected in the thing, something for all the naysayers to latch on to. I told that Englishman George Moore that I had discovered the true color of air is violet. I wanted to say something sensational to him, since that was evidently what he expected from me, but it was an actual truth I told him: the air is violet. I saw so that day that Léon and I walked along the river in the midst of all the dragonflies. Everyone will fault me for the impossible color—they will say I have lost my mind entirely. Manet the crackpot. So be it. They will be so busy talking about that wine-colored air of the painting that they will be forced to look upon the real story being told.

I made Pertuiset red. His face is florid above his whiskers, his hands pink and meaty. All that purple and red—what a contrast against the tawny lion.

THE LAST FEW NIGHTS when spasms came, I pressed my heel against the wall as hard as I could and pretended it was the red octopus squeezing me. For some ridiculous reason it kept me sane.

My octopus is straight from Hokusai—red head and spherical eyes. Fearsome and erotic both.

UNLIKELY—THAT WAS WHAT Tonin rated my chances of success at the Salon with either of the Rochefort paintings. When I reminded him that amnesty had been declared and that Rochefort was now regarded as some kind of hero, he said, "That may be. But the Salon jury will be divided at best about lauding a prison escape."

"Then I will send this," I told him, and gestured to the Pertuiset.

I give Tonin credit—he did not respond for some time. And when he did, all he said was, "I'm not sure I follow you here."

I let him go on looking at the pinks and violets until his eyes were fully saturated. Then I took his arm and, without saying anything, made him stand in front of the life-sized *Execution of Maximilian*, rehung so that one's face is on level with the faces in the painting, with those being executed and the executioners.

Tonin is not new to the work, but he studied it anew, bending to look at Maximilian grasping the hand of Miramón.

"It always disturbs me," he said. "It doesn't matter how many times I see it."

In a moment, he started to say something else, but I held up my hand. Walked him instead to the table, where I had laid out my old sketches of the soldiers and bodies at the barricades.

"It is all the same story," I said. "Don't you see? All of them. To the victor go the spoils," I said.

"Pertuiset is not in the same vein."

"Yes, he is, Tonin. David and Goliath exist only in the Bible. The one with the best gun always wins."

He looked over everything again. Walked from Maximilian to Pertuiset to the drawings and back again.

"They won't see it," he told me, shaking his head.

"You can't see it unless you see all the pieces side by side," I said. "I know. But it doesn't matter. I know it's there."

"If people could see your work. See the range and the breadth of it," he said, and gestured. "The sheer size of the Maximillian alone. That terror bearing down on you. It is criminal that you were prevented from exhibiting it."

Supportive as always! But I think he understood for the first time what I meant when I told him I did not want to go into museums or exhibitions piecemeal. It was something we talked about last year when I was painting his portrait, when he waxed on about what a triumph it would be to get *Olympia* or *Père Lathuille* into the Luxembourg. I think he was hurt when I shut him down and told him I did not want a single painting, or even a couple, to represent me.

I would not be whole, I told him.

I was so vehement about it at the time. He agreed with me just to end the awkwardness, but I was sure he did not understand. Now, with the help of Pertuiset, lion hunter, he understands.

"I stand behind you. I always do."

"You walk in their world much more successfully than I do," I said. "I take your opinion to heart."

Because it is an achievement, too: to be wholly understood by one person. He should have been my father's son. My father would have been proud of his career in a way he never could be of mine.

We stood in front of Maximilian then, looking at that impossible blond head waiting for death. Tonin gripped my arm and did not let go for a long time. My oldest schoolboy friend.

ROCHEFORT COMES TOMORROW, but only after I sent off another note to him, imploring. "Do not deny me this opportunity," I wrote, "to make your portrait for all of Paris to see." I told him I would try do it all in one go, so as not to waste his "precious hours."

An impossible claim, but somehow I will do the thing I promised. I will get the heart of him in the first sitting and fill in from photographs if I need to. And I will paint him in the pose of Clemenceau—"so the world may see another side to the Republic!"

Who knows? If I sit staring at him long enough, perhaps I will pierce that shell of his. It happens that way sometimes. One sits in a still room with a person, and after that initial awkwardness drops away—after everyone settles into the time and the space—a different thing begins to happen. Façades drop, faces soften, natural silences emerge, along with revelations. I think it is a natural consequence of being seen—people feel noticed. Understood. Or not—some cannot bear it. But others feel compelled to share secrets, or they go into a private space all their own, especially if they do not have to return my gaze.

But something happens in me, too. I settle into the session, certainly—but I mean something begins to alter in my perceptions of that person. I sense them differently, get a feeling for the whole of them. If they let me. With some people it is instantaneous, as it was with Trine and Mèry, and with others it develops over time—Berthe. With Tonin it is just the old intimacy that has always been there.

And certainly it is easier with women, but it does not happen with all women. I could never get a sense of Eva Gonzalès. How many times did I scrape away the paint of her face? At first I thought it was because she was my pupil, that I was attempting to demonstrate something to her instead of simply painting—but it was more than that. I could not get beyond the shell of her, could not ever see her entirety. And if I am honest, the same was true of La Lemonnier. There was always a flatness there.

Is it just that one loves some faces immediately?

I loved Léon's face as a little boy, and the soft burr of his hair. But I also loved the face of that boy who used to help me in my studio on rue de Douai the one who killed himself. There was something about the paleness of his skin and the fairness of his hair, like a little sun shining in his eagerness for everything. Then finding him like that, hanging from a thin cord—all these years later I cannot let myself think too much about it. If I go down that path in my thoughts it is too difficult to return.

Sharing the still air of the studio with another person—it is an intimacy. Then the painting ends and that person goes away. And you have to let the intimacy end.

ROCHEFORT MADE IT CLEAR he was granting a favor—but I am not sure it was to me. Perhaps it was a favor to future generations who should not be deprived of this likeness of Rochefort, the hero!

When Clemenceau crossed his arms over his chest, he looked as if he were waiting. Uncomfortably, perhaps, but for the duration. Rochefort, on the other hand, appeared to be stopped in transit, pausing only. And yet—I caught a pensive quality. As if he were remembering, or seeing something only he could perceive. And his façade never lifted. There was no small talk. I worked and he gazed at something only he saw. No matter—at some point something in his face softened. He gave me that.

At the end of the time, he did ask about the painting of his sea escape. "Out being framed," I told him.

He nodded. "Some other time, then," he said, but I did not detect any real curiosity in him. I think he was glad to be spared having to respond to my work in any way.

I fully intended to show him both versions of the scene, the one in which he was the star and the other, in which the sea took center stage. I intended to hear out his opinion. But at the last minute I put both canvases in the interior room. If he saw them and said anything unpleasant, I knew it would derail me for the portrait. I could not risk it.

Victor Henri Rochefort, Marquis de Rochefort-Luçay. If I caught something of the man, it was only by luck.

I SHOULD HAVE INCLUDED *Rue Mosnier with Flags*, the one with the one-legged veteran on his crutches, when I gave Tonin that tour the other day. That is the cost of flag-waving and wars. If the only way I can make that point at the Salon is through Pertuiset, I will take it. Human or lion, neither of us can stand against a bullet. We are both corpses in the end.

And that one-legged man in a blue coat on rue Mosnier? I am he and he is me. I just did not know it at the time.

I SHOULD STOP READING *Le Figaro*.

Boy with a Sword sold for 9,100 fr. to Jules Feder. It sounds like a decent enough sum, but it was actually the lowest sale on the list. A Delacroix went for 95,000 fr., and a couple of Rousseaus fetched nearly 50,000 fr. each.

And all that might be borne more easily if I had not originally sold *Boy* back in '72 for just 1,200 fr. But that is the marketplace. One sells when one needs to sell, as one can sell. Needs must and all that.

Turquet bought one of the Rousseaus for the Louvre. He must not know a bargain when he sees it; he could have had my awkward boy with a sword for just one-fifth of that sum!

THEY ARE GONE, the paintings of Pertuiset and Rochefort. Sent off to be judged. For the twenty-second time I approach that altar.

As much as I love the whaleboat and the endless waves of the paintings of Rochefort's escapes, I sent the traditional portrait of him in his black coat. Let the jury judge Rochefort the man, not the escaping prisoner. There is a gravitas in the figure in the portrait, in the expression on his face, and I dare anyone to claim otherwise.

As for Pertuiset, let them make of it what they will. It was my choice to send it. My submission to waste.

SPRING MUST BE COMING. When I walked to the studio this morning, a boulevard loafer leaned against a *chasse-roue* along Batignolles, enjoying the air. He was still there when I came home, just farther down the street, following the path of the sun.

PEOPLE ARE TALKING ABOUT the Rochefort portrait in the same way they talked about *A Good Glass of Beer* so long ago. I do not see the connection between the two works, but I will take the approval.

Apparently even Sireday is pressing my case. He stopped by to see me the other day when Tonin was here, and he took Tonin to task.

"You are the minister of the fine arts," Sireday told him. "Can't you see to it that one of these paintings is bought for the state?"

Ephrussi bought the *Pickle Jar* the other day—another homely little painting—and Duret's friend Deudon bought *Plum Brandy*. That constitutes a run for me, I think.

I am like the girl that no one asked to dance and who suddenly has a full card.

Glad for the sales but part of me was sad to see the plum girl go—she was with me a long time. My sister and my fellow wanderer, a modern Aphrodite in a pink dress instead of on a half shell.

DINNER AT NITTIS'S again tonight. I had pain all day and should not have gone, but I like him so much that I did not want to say no.

And the distraction was good for me, at least for a time. But Goncourt began to wear on me even faster than usual—his oily voice, always making pronouncements. At a certain point the only way I could keep my mind engaged was to tell a story I heard from one of my models.

"She was a young woman at the time," I began. "And when her grandmother died, of course she grieved. The old woman had been especially kind to her. She gave the girl her first real toy, a tiny stuffed rabbit."

I made the story last as long as I could, telling about the girl's fatigue during the long Catholic mass for her grandmother, and about how she got waylaid at the end of the service when she had to go back inside and retrieve her muff.

"She was just thirteen at the time and wasn't used to pretty things like that. She'd borrowed the muff from her neighbor especially for the church service. When she finally came outside again, the only spot for her in a funeral carriage was with an elderly great-uncle. The ride started off innocently enough, with chatting about the old woman that girl loved so much. But the uncle was not at all a nice old man, and he used the time in the carriage to deflower the girl."

"That was the beginning of her education on the nature of men," Paul Bourget said.

"When I asked this young woman if she was angry at her great-uncle for what he had done, she said yes and no," I told them then. "She said she hated him at the time, but that he died soon after and left her some money, which she greatly needed. 'That is one meaning of the phrase blood money, don't you think?' she asked me, and I could only nod."

They all think models have no morals at all, so they gobbled up the story like so many hungry chickens. All except La Dame de Nitti, who looked embarrassed and pained.

I did not last long in that company after my tale, and when Mme de Nitti walked me to the door, I said, "It was a foul story to tell. I offended you, and I am sorry."

"It entertained some," she said. "And I saw that it took your mind off things."

Am I that transparent in my pain?

A MEDAL. A SALON MEDAL. With it, the honor of hors concours hereafter. Never to be judged again by a jury, my works accepted without question.

Henri Gervex came to tell me.

"I wanted to be the one to deliver the news," he said. "I came as quickly as I could."

"I see that, my friend," after the initial disbelief. "Sit and rest."

"I hardly can, friend, for rejoicing. I would not be who I am were it not for you."

"You would have found your way," I told him. "But I appreciate your sentiment all the same."

As he was leaving, late for another appointment, Tonin arrived. When I turned to greet him, I stumbled a bit, and Gervex caught me—I think it was the shock of the whole thing making me clumsier than usual. Tonin made his way to me then, and the three of us stood together for a moment, their arms linked loosely with mine until they were sure I was steady. A triad.

"He is genuinely moved," Tonin said of Gervex after he left. "He fought hard for you on the jury. It was not unanimous."

I wanted to tell him that I thought of Gervex as a son—he was born the same year as Léon. But I did not want to sound patronizing, so I just said, "I believe that."

We sat drinking the bottle of wine Tonin brought with him. He let me say things, over and over. And he repeated every bit of the gossip he heard, some bits several times—and yet it was still difficult for me to believe. A Salon medal. For me. You wait for something all your life, and when it arrives, you hardly know what to think, or how to think. You need to have someone tell you the news again and again.

"You said there were no first-class medals given, only seconds. Why was that?" I asked Tonin after the thing had sunk in a bit. "Did the jury not deem anything worthy?"

"It was a strategy, Édouard. Carefully planned."

I nodded—and then I understood.

"Because of me."

"Because members of the jury wanted to redress a wrong that has existed too long. An injustice. That is how strongly your supporters on the jury felt. Every artist worthy of an award received the same recognition as you, which alone makes a statement. And no one could argue about taking away your award without making their agenda plain."

We sat quietly, and I let the thing sink in again.

"I hardly know what to say," I told Tonin. "The advance planning it took—"

"They were determined, Édouard. Gervex had a strategy, and he executed it."

"Then I owe him an even larger debt."

"You do not owe anyone anything. You paved the way for many."

"I did not, Tonin. I wanted recognition for myself. Year after year, I sent to the Salon only work I wanted to send. I had no agenda other than a personal one."

"That is precisely it. You advocated for the unique and the personal. Not the fashionable. Not the officially sanctioned."

I shook my head then. It was too much to consider.

"I will take the thing at face value," I said. "A second-class medal. And in the future, free to show what I please, as I please."

We looked at each other for a long second and then I had to look away. And Tonin did me the great service of offering up all the conversation he had so I could sit there in stunned silence, needing only to smile and nod and laugh, all my thoughts silent inside me, but simmering just the same.

LAVIEILLE, VOLLON, DUEZ, CAZIN, Gervex, Carolus-Duran, Bin, Roll, Feyen-Perrin, Guillaumet, Vuillefroy, Guillemet, Émile Lévy, Lansyer, Lalanne, Henner, de Neuville—those are the jurors that voted for me to receive a second-class medal for the portrait of Rochefort.

De Neuville wrote me this morning to say the medal was only "just," and proof of the "sincerity and personality" of my talent. He also confessed he tried but could not persuade his comrades to award me the Cross of the Legion of Honor immediately—they feared it would ignite criticism and might backfire entirely. They decided it was sufficiently provocative to award the second-class medal and allow the decoration to come later at the scheduled time. Perhaps De Neuville fears I will not be around long enough to receive the Cross if they delay, but I am here and I intend to stay here.

The count was seventeen in favor of my award to sixteen against— Tonin did not exaggerate when he told me I had trimmed my sails close. I still cause an uproar, and my name still sticks in the craw for some—like Cabanel. He apparently spoke in favor of my portrait of Pertuiset to his fellow jurors, but when the vote came, he could not bring himself to support me! I will not forget that. I want to say something rich and scathing about it all, but I cannot. I am joyous. Nothing dilutes it.

I will pay a visit to each one of the jurors who voted yes. By hook or by crook and with my cane, I will go.

NOTES, VISITS, FLOWERS—NEWS SPREADS. Some seem as startled as I am, but everyone, at least those who come to see me or write, appears wholly pleased and joyful. In a simple note, Ephrussi said, *A lifetime in the making.* That is the phrase I keep repeating in my mind.

And this morning I felt myself rise above my life. I can suddenly take the long view on everything. I see the reasons for everything, my mistakes as well as my successes, and I understand my choices. Instead of castigating myself as I do so often, I feel able to see each decision as a stepping-stone, a point along a path. Perhaps it is a false view, but I will take it. It is a relief to see my actions as efforts to survive instead of desperation. Even the '67 show, so debilitating in its costs, now seems crucial. I mounted it because I thought it was the thing to do, because I needed to do *something.* And I did do something.

I survived.

But now that I have this medal, this recognition, what comes next? That is the only real question. *What next?*

I DO NOT KNOW whether to laugh or cry over the letter from Duez.

First he informs me that the portrait of Pertuiset with his gun was "a push" for the jurors to endorse, and that it made some grind their teeth. So be it! The portrait was meant to be a push, and I do not back down from it. But after telling me that, Duez ends his missive by saying that I should be "consoled" by everything that happened, and that the second-class medal proves that I am "alive and kicking."

So they just wanted to give me a medal before I died. Maybe the whole thing was an act of sympathy—I cannot rule that out. Or perhaps I got the medal for stubbornness and tenacity.

For the twenty-one times I went before them with my best work, with honest and sincere work.

For the tirades that followed me year after year.

For coming back to try again and again, even when I got sent home with my tail between my legs.

For giving them all, every last one of them, something to talk about year in and year out. If it wasn't *Luncheon on the Grass,* it was *Olympia*; if it wasn't my flat use of unrealistic color, it was the sketchy quality of my painting. People even found a way to criticize the dog Victorine kept on her lap in *Gare Saint-Lazare*. Some fool called it a seal. Nothing was too small to escape their lambasting.

Make it true, let people talk—I have lived that motto every day. Even when every comment someone made felt like a blow, even when nothing felt at all alive inside me. I live that motto even now when the main thing alive in me is this rotting disease.

So yes, maybe I did get the medal because I am still alive. And I will take the medal for goddamn still being alive.

Paris   1 APRIL 1881

MÉRY CAME TODAY. Of course she is happy for me—she can enter
fully into someone else's joy because she is happy.

It was enough to lie together on the divan, talking.

I AM FATIGUED TODAY. I do not know why it surprises me. For days I felt buoyed by news of the medal, and I am buoyed still, but it does not mean my pain has vanished. Today my legs twist and jerk, and my feet seem like two overtightened knobs.

And here I am, describing the thing I said I would no longer describe. Still, it gives Mind something to do, a way to speak for its poor, dumb brother Body.

I TRIED SOMETHING new today.

When the pain started in my left leg, I purposely imagined an octopus wrapping itself over the worst spot. I pictured the oval head over the worst of the stabbing. Not a red octopus this time but a glowing lavender one, cool-fleshed and sinuous.

It did not stop the pain or lessen its intensity. But the duration of the worst spasms seemed shorter—maybe because I was not working to label the pain with images of heat or knives. I imagined that the lavender tentacles wrapped around me, covered with viscous moisture, held the chill of the Atlantic. This cool plum creature of the oceans soothed me.

Now that I write it out, it seems so obvious. *I need images of chilled water and the sea to combat my pain.*

OF COURSE THE MEDAL has come too late. If it had happened fifteen years ago, or ten. Even five. But would I have painted any other way? Painted different subjects? Allowed myself greater freedoms?

I painted what I wanted. But maybe I would have lived with less doubt. Shame and doubt, the two great cripplers—greater even than this disease.

At least my paintings were shameless, even if I was not.

THE WHOLE IDEA THAT I wrote about here yesterday, that I might have painted differently if I had felt less doubt, is beside the point. The only thing that matters is that I painted what I could, as I could.

Yes, I made choices. I followed my passions and predilections. But after a certain point, there is only one way. One tries different aspects, versions, angles—even different faces. But what one *arrives at* is all that matters. I painted the only way I could paint. There was no choice, in that sense.

This is more true for some paintings than others. Yes, there are two versions of Rochefort's *Escape*, and multiple versions of *The Execution of Maximilian*. But there was only one *Olympia*. It took me years to find her face, and without Victorine, I could not have discovered it. And yet it was not Trine's face in the painting in the end. It was something separate, something that belonged to the painting and to the painting alone.

Things choose me. And when they do not, sometimes they are failures.

The portrait of Eva Gonzalès at her easel failed, and the original dead toreador failed before I cut the canvas into pieces. One completes these tableaux, but they never have the life they are meant to have.

What do I mean that things choose me?

I mean there is a life force that comes out from people, but also from things, that makes me want to paint. It feels like the vibration of a tuning fork. I grow conscious. Like a rabbit or a bird or a salamander when it realizes a human is nearby, watching, I realize I am in the presence of something. And not just living beings—the whaleboat has a presence and a life force, too. After so many years on the sea, of carrying and giving chase, of course it has a life force. It absorbed it from above and below.

People say artists have an eye for things. Of course it is true. You see a scrap of something and it becomes more. It informs. But it is more than just having an eye for things—you get the breath of things. Sometimes the air around a person or a flower can vibrate with life.

Even when I am asked to paint or draw something, commissioned to do so, I try to find the angle that resonates with me. It can be anything. The smallest detail can engage me. In the past few days, the tuning fork has been set off by

~A single stalk of chicory blooming in the courtyard
~A woman on Batignolles with pockmarks on her cheeks that made her look so fierce, they were the heart of her beauty

It is either a failing or my best quality that it takes so little to interest me.

EPHRUSSI STOPPED BY WITH the print I asked him to loan me—Hokusai's *Dream of the Fisherman's Wife*.

"I can't stay," he told me. "But I wanted you to have it quickly. I didn't want to delay your plans."

I was glad he wanted to get away—I did not want to have to make polite conversation with him, all the while trying to keep my mind from the print he was loaning me. A *shunga* image of two octopuses ravishing a woman, I am sure he thinks my plans are for some kind of erotic art. But I mainly want to look at the thing and study it *as medicine*. I want to study the way Hokusai drew these octopuses so I can better imagine the rainbow creatures I apply as poultices to the worst of my pain.

I seem to assign different roles to the octopuses based on color.

The original iridescent red octopus is a battler, and a warning. I use it for the worst spasms, its grip strong and unrelenting.

The lavender and purple ones have a cooling effect, as does a mossy green one.

I picture midnight-blue octopuses when I get a particular stabbing feeling in my heels.

I save the ink-black giant octopus for when it seems my whole body is wracked. When that comes, I am not sure if I picture the octopus attached to me, or if I crawl inside it—I let everything go black and swirling with seawater and ink.

Recently I have added a tiny pearlescent octopuses. They cling delicately to my fingers when I feel pins and needles in my hands.

PEOPLE DO KEEP USING the word "plans." Not just Ephrussi the other day—I mean friends and acquaintances want to know what the Salon medal means to me, what I will do now that I have it, what I plan to do.

I plan to go on doing what I did before. What else would I do? It is not as if I were leading some alternate and preparatory life up until this point.

Still, I know what they mean. But the truth is I do not know. I do not know what the next *Olympia* or *Maximilian* is—only that it will not be like either of those works. Things should never be the same.

Paris 25 APRIL 1881

NO HYDROPATHY THIS SUMMER—only rest. That is the word from Sireday. On the one hand it seems like giving up. But it is also a relief because the treatments cost so much and were so enervating.

Yet they were meant to enervate. I would endure it all again if he or Materne thought it would do any good! But if that is not the case, if the effect is so doubtful, then—

I would as soon spend the summer in Gennevilliers as anywhere, but Sireday says the humidity will do me no good, and Jules is ensconced there with all of his ills. How many springs have I missed the peonies flowering at Gennevilliers, and the white lilacs? Too many.

YESTERDAY WHEN I SAW Sireday I told him my theory that everything with this disease began back in '71.

"I remember your symptoms well, Édouard," he said. "In all likelihood, the true beginning and initial infection would have occurred anywhere from two weeks to a year earlier. And, of course, secondary syphilis can recur."

Doctors are marshals of death, all of them. You tell them your intimate secrets, and they use them to dissect and break you down further.

WE WILL SPEND THE summer in Versailles, courtesy of M. Bernstein, who has found us a house to rent. I have no enthusiasm for the plan.

I SENT OFF A PAINTING for the sale benefitting Cabaner at l'Hôtel Drouot—*The Suicide*, of all things. It fetched just 65 fr., so it will not pay for much of his bills.

I think people did not know what to make of it. By sending such a work, I am sure some believed I selfishly wanted to cause a sensation even at such a somber affair, but that is not true. It would be wrong to say I did not anticipate the reaction, but that is different than saying I wanted to cause the reaction. Or who knows, perhaps it was in poor taste that I sent this particular painting for a friend who is suffering.

The only death that is "suitable" to paint is a war death, a glorious death in battle. Yet most of us die as Cabaner is dying, from a disease that happens bit by bit. There is no way to paint such an ordeal in a realistic way, so no one paints the most common kind of death at all. We tell greater truths about the death of flowers than we do about our own. When someone dares to show even the honest aftereffects of death, as Courbet did in *A Burial at Ornans*, he is excoriated for it.

But it seems to me suicide is its own kind of "death in battle," and it may stand in for all of our sufferings—for Cabaner's, too.

People commit suicide when they are at war with sadness, or fear, or loneliness, or pain. When a single blow seems preferable to daily assault. Suicide is not heroic, nor romantic, nor idealistic, but neither is it cowardly or sinful. Made in a fit of passion or very deliberately, it is a choice. Tonin and I talk about it sometimes—we both understand the desperation that might lead to it, and we both wonder if we would be able to take such a step.

It is a choice I wish Cabaner could have if he so desired it: an end to suffering. It is a choice that belongs to all men, and to all women. It pains me to say it, but the choice belonged to my studio assistant when he was just a boy. It belongs to me.

If I had wanted to shock I would have painted wasted limbs, jaundiced skin, oozing sores, the heavy sweat of fever. I would have painted myself holding my foot like a contortionist, my face a rictus of agony. Instead I painted a moment in time, and an action about which we may have private thoughts. I painted the interior of our minds—and that is what I gave for Cabaner

WHAT USE IS MODERNITY if it is not willing to tell a new story? I am still turning over stones in my mind about *The Suicide*, and that is what I keep coming to. What use is all the emphasis on the new and the modern if we are so afraid to tell the stories that are current? Our own stories?

We have all known sorrow and despair, so how can that painting be foreign to so many, and so unacceptable? A man has come to the end of his tether and decided to end the misery. What could be more straightforward or universal? Does it really matter why he committed suicide?

When people must decide something for themselves, they panic. They want instead a story that is immediately recognizable, and that immediacy is key. Yet in the truly modern, you sometimes have to take the time to decide and decipher. The time in front of the work is crucial. Yet that makes people uncomfortable, too. They *have to* stand in front of a naked woman with no uplifting myth or ideal—someone that they might see in the street. They *have to* look upon a desperate man alone in a room, someone who looks like them or someone they know. And that is unbearable.

Modernity requires time in front of the painting to decide its meaning. Modernity requires a truthful narrative of the self, whatever it might be. Modernity requires new narratives that we must learn to perceive and understand on their own terms.

When I paint "modern life," I include the viewer in the front of the canvas, and the time he or she must take to perceive the canvas. It is why *Olympia* looks out directly and forthrightly, and why there are no "clues" offered in *The Suicide*. I not only make time for the viewer to observe the painting and make a decision, I demand it.

So speaks Manet to a crowd of none.

I DO NOT KNOW why I am thinking of her.

Is it all the thinking about *Olympia* these past days? My own despair as reflected in *The Suicide*?

All I know is I remembering the days I used to go down and wait for Trine outside Baudon, how I loafed in the street, smoking, waiting until the moment when the big side door of the factory would open and all the women would come pouring out, talking and laughing. And then I would see her and Denise, the two of them, redhead and brunette, slipping out of their aprons, walking toward me, walking until they were beside me, and each would take an arm, and they'd call back over their shoulders to friends, bantering, and then that would stop and it would just be the three of us, the three of us, and we would set off—first for dinner, always for dinner, because that was crucial: that I fill their bellies, that I always fill their bellies and take away hunger for as long as we were all three of us together.

And then after I fed them, we would walk and walk, and I never got over the delight of it, the frisson of the feeling of having a girl on each arm, a forearm wrapping each of my forearms, a breast pressed against each side of me, warm and full, and I felt rich, richer than any man had a right to be, and they were such good friends, so close and loving. I loved them, too, the two of them, Trine with her furious silences and Denise always so polite and obliging, and it hurt me to know I drove a wedge between them. It hurt me but I could not quit them, and yet when Trine chose me, and when she demanded that I choose her, I did so willingly, and I lost my beautiful brunette Denise, but I chose and was happy with my choice, happy that a young woman loved me so openly. And whoever says that artists choose their muses is foolish, my muse chose me, a working girl with rough hands and dirty feet chose me, and my life and my art changed forever, and if I have this medal today or any day that is to come it is partly because of Trine, Victorine—

THE FLOOD AT TOULOUSE, *The Old Quarryman*, *Fête of Silenus*, yes, but mostly *The Miners' Strike*, exhibited last year with a power few could approach—that was all I knew of Alfred Philippe Roll, one of the young artists that Duez said supported me in the vote, and whom I was determined to visit and thank personally. Now I hardly have the words to describe the friendship he showed me today.

He and his friend the English painter Alfred Smith were waiting outside his studio when I arrived. The two of them greeted me with such warmth, with long handshakes and such a grasping of my arms, smiling the whole time, exclaiming and beaming.

"What an honor and an incredible joy," Roll said.

"The joy is mine," I told him.

When we came inside, I saw they had laid a small table with wine and food and understood they meant to celebrate with me. At first it was hard for me to know how to respond to their mirth and energy, but they made it easy, asking questions and listening intently. When it became so one-sided I felt embarrassed, I asked Roll to show me around, and he did, including Smith's works, whom he was in the process of advocating for.

"It makes a tremendous difference, doesn't it?" I said, looking at Smith. "One person who understands you and champions you?"

After Roll translated for him, Smith nodded and said, "Oui, Monsieur Manet."

I turned to Roll then and said, "I want to thank you for all that you did for me."

"I did what was right."

He again grasped my hand and held on to it. It was a pleasure to look into his frank and open face.

I think I must have done something of value to have the admiration of someone like him or Gervex. Maybe I have not been as alone as I thought I was.

How is it that strangers sometimes support you more than your friends? No, that is not wholly true—no one could be more loyal than Tonin. Maybe it is simply that you rely so heavily on old friends that their voices in your head begin to sound like your own, and when you hear a new friend's words, they fall like fresh rain.

FOR SOME REASON ALL spasms stopped as soon as I got into bed last night. I had pain, yes, but the jumping of my muscles ceased, and the endless tics. I waited awhile and then I got up and went to S's room.

"I can go if it's too much," I said in the darkness.

"It's fine," she said, shifting on the bed. Making room for me.

I sleep like an old log sometimes when I am with her. Something about her breathing, about the familiar weight of her beside me. She is the animal I know best in this world.

Before I crawled onto the bed I checked for Jicky. He was in between S's legs, up by her crotch in that warm nook. He hadn't given up his spot even when she moved.

So the three of us slept.

I TOOK ADVANTAGE OF the relative absence of pain and jerking and walked farther this morning than I have in weeks.

When I looked out into people's faces, it seemed as if I knew them all. I thought, if only I could observe them a little longer, if only they would slow or stop, I would be able to place them all, and connect them with whatever corner of life I knew them from. I kept waiting to hear my name or see recognition break over someone's features when they saw me.

I think it is a sign of my hunger for life outside the studio and home. Or else my mind is playing tricks on me, and my vision is becoming as impaired as my legs.

The sensation of somehow knowing everyone stayed with me for the whole of my walk. All those faces and lives—

ANOTHER VISIT TO A member of the Salon jury: Félix Vuillefroy has a species of Spanish ground beetle named after him, *Nebria vuillefroyi*. He found it in 1865.

"It changed the course of my life," he said. "I left behind a career of dusty folders and began to study with the greatest of all teachers, Nature."

When I thanked him for his help in voting, he seemed so uncomfortable that I said my piece and stopped. We then spent the afternoon talking about his two great passions, insects and cows, and I think I conveyed my appreciation better that way, by listening intently, than with any words.

And it was wholly pleasant to see dozens of paintings and engravings of cows. When I told him that I loved the placid feeling the works gave me, he smiled.

"People always use that word to describe cows. But they're also joyful creatures. They run and play, and they love music."

I believed him. I did! But I did not know what to say to that statement. So I said the one thing that came to my mind.

"Perhaps my wife can play for cows this summer."

"They would love that," Vuillefroy told me. So I guess it was not a stupid thing to say.

When he saw me to the door, he shook my hand again and said, "Nature heals." He did not look down at my cane or my leg, but I understood. But he spoke with such profound emotion I could not bristle.

"I hope you are right," I said.

A true fanatic, he gives off a bit of the air of a madman. But afterward, I also felt strangely peaceful. He is a great cow priest, Vuillefroy, and I have been inside his church.

SOMETHING HAS SHIFTED IN the past week.

Sometime during the night after I paid my visit to Vuillefroy, the big toe on my left foot took on a life of its own. Alternately, it felt as if it were being scalded in boiling water, or as if someone were trying to wrench it from my foot. I went through two days of that and then broke down and sent word to Sireday.

Yet even on the laudanum he prescribed, I cannot bear to have even a sheet touch it. Yesterday I somehow thought it was slightly better, so I attempted to put on a sock—and that was disastrous. As soon as the fabric went over my skin, my whole leg lit up.

And so this morning I sent Léon to the studio to pick up a few things, including this notebook. I am back in bed again, sweating, stripped down to my underwear with my left calf elevated on a pillow so my foot can dangle out in the open air.

I DO NOT KNOW why I wanted this notebook so badly—I feel as though I have nothing on my mind except my foot. Still, just having this book is a comfort. I like looking back through its pages.

MY TOE IS LESS PAINFUL. One might think that is a relief. But I have no sensation in most of that foot now.

I can tell I have a foot—I can feel that something is present where my foot was, and I can still feel my heel. But if I touch my toe, I cannot feel my fingers. Not even if I pinch. Not even when Sireday pokes with a needle.

He came in here to take a bath and fall asleep.

DESPITE THE MEDAL AND the vigorous championing by some of my fellows, the reviews of my paintings are no different than I expected.

Mantz says Rochefort is badly painted, and that Pertuiset is awash in a "winy atmosphere."

Fourcaud writes that my portrait is the equivalent of a slap in the face to Rochefort. Furthermore, he is personally "insulted" that I am to be awarded even a second-place medal, since I am a painter of slapped-together clichés and "the grotesque."

That word always makes it in somehow. Someone really wants to say that he finds *me* grotesque, but if he says that, he might appear to be unfair. So instead he characterizes my vision and my ability to find all that is hideous in the world. I am grotesque by association, but the critic remains perceptive and upright.

Huysmans writes that he is "seriously contrite" about being obliged to judge me so harshly, but alas, he has to be true to himself and the public. Then he delivers his verdicts: Pertuiset appears as if he were out hunting rabbits and not lions, and I make the esteemed face of Rochefort look like cheese pie the birds have been pecking at.

I guess he would not have found my Batignolles woman appealing with her good-looking pockmarks.

So the medal changes nothing. People see exactly what they have always seen in me. A few understand but many still excoriate; the ratio has not changed. The only thing that changed is that a few who understand have come into some power. And they battered the walls on my behalf.

AMONG ALL THE LETTERS and notes of congratulations from well-wishers, one is conspicuous by its absence: there is nothing from Rochefort.

Of course I have heard things. He finds the portrait juvenile. Primitive. He disapproves entirely.

So be it. I painted what I saw. His uncompromising face. The way his frock coat pulled across his arms. His impatience with me and with the world itself.

TODAY IS THE SALON awards ceremony. Of course I will stay home. We leave for Versailles tomorrow, so today there are preparations—but I do not want to hear the cacophony when my name is announced. Mostly I do not want to limp in. So once again I cut myself off from things.

It is something that hit me that afternoon with Vuillefroy—how much I have missed because I have wanted to protect myself. It seems an entirely natural response, and I have not been without friends and allies. But I cut myself off from a whole range of interaction with men such as Félix Vuillefroy. I assumed he was like the other Academy painters.

But no one is like anyone else. Or, one may be a member of a cadre and also stand apart from it.

Which is not to say I was wrong about things—sixteen voted against me. Almost a majority. So I had, and have, my reasons for sticking with my ragtag bunch of friends and allies.

THE HOUSE—WELL, IT WILL DO. The garden is an afterthought. Empty trellises everywhere.

But one end of the lane at the back of the house abuts a fenced field, and I think I saw cows pastured there—I saw it when the trap brought us here. When I said as much to S this morning, she looked at me. "Since when are you interested in cows?" she asked.

"Since I met with Vuillefroy. He told me they are joyful creatures that love music."

"Of course they love music. Most animals do."

"How do you know that about cows? I never heard of it before Vuillefroy."

"Everyone in Bommel knew. I wish I could take a piano outside. I would go and play for them."

She said this as naturally as anything, over a piece of bread and jam.

Versailles

EVENING PRIMROSE, CAMPION, MARGUERITE, CHICORY, pimpernel—and a small herd of four cows. That is what S and I saw when we walked down to the fenced meadow across the lane behind the house. There is a small line of trees at the far end of the field that we cannot see beyond, and it may be that there are more cows beyond the trees. But there are at least four, and they seemed to look in our direction when they realized we were there.

DESIGNED BY LE NÔTRE, the Versailles gardens and grounds at the palace are magnificent—or so I am told. I tried to walk some of it with Léon yesterday and failed.

The paths were smooth but it did not matter—my dragging foot could not cover a fraction of those distances. When I looked ahead and realized just how far everything was, branching out and out, I got an episode of dizzying vertigo, the same as came over me at Christmas.

Léon helped me to a bench, and we waited a good half hour until I thought I could move again. On the ride home I used all my strength and focus not to vomit.

"We can try another day when you feel stronger," Léon said.

I did not answer—did not even shake my head for fear of risking the movement of my head.

The fact is that I have lost almost all feeling in my left foot. I have none at all in the toes, and very little around the heel. I do not feel the ground when I walk, can no longer move my foot in anything approaching a normal manner. To walk at all, I lift my leg up from the hip and swing it forward, and I only know I have made the step if I look down, or when I hear my foot slap the ground.

I can will myself to walk short distances, so that is what I will do. I will content myself painting this garden, with its empty trellises and its gobs of flowers. I will do all that I can still do.

WORKING ON AN OIL of a green bench in the garden. I have so little interest in it I will be surprised if I finish.

A BIT OF DRIZZLE this morning but I went out anyway. The garden is too depressing even in good weather, so I walked around the back of the house to the lane, where a clump of thistles is growing. I was just beginning to think of how people malign thistles and then I saw it: an upside-down bumblebee under the pink head of a thistle.

I expected it to fly off as I approached, but it stayed in the same spot, even as I bent down to look at it. That is when I realized the bumblebee was asleep under the umbrella of the thistle. I stood there for a while longer, and then I came in to get my pastels.

TODAY WHEN LÉON CAME, he was carrying a small black case. When I asked what it was, he said, "My old fife. You said last week you wanted to play music to the cows."

I must have looked completely blank, because S said, "You do remember he had a fife."

"I remember the fife I used as a prop."

"Don't you remember Léon playing it?"

"I remember him tootling on it."

Léon looked at S and then at me. "Well, I thought we could try it on your cows," he said.

So after lunch the three of us traipsed down to the field, with S carrying the case, and Léon with me and my cane on one arm, and carrying a chair with the other hand.

The cows were at the far end of the meadow, near the trees. I could not tell if they saw us or not. Léon looked at them and then down at the fife.

"I don't know if the sound will carry that far," he said.

"Go ahead and try," S told him.

So he played a few notes, and then he played a simple song. Hesitating in places, but an actual tune. I did not know what to watch—him playing, or the cows as they began to move across the field.

The longer Léon played, the surer he grew of the song. Six cows—all that had been standing at the trees—picked their way through the grass to the fence, where they stood in a cluster. They looked at Léon and us and each other, they bowed and bobbed their heads and turned to twitch at flies or look off over their backs and at each other—but they never moved away.

Léon played the same song several times through, for a matter of minutes. Then he stopped and handed the fife to S so he could get a handkerchief from his pocket and wipe his forehead. The cows watched his every move, shifting a bit in their group but still occupying their ground.

"They're waiting to see what you do next," S told him.

"I'll play again in a bit," Léon said, as much to his red and white audience as to the two of us.

And I sat in quiet astonishment at it all.

I THINK EVERYTHING HAS been backward for me. Help has come from younger men, not older.

Maybe it is because we talk primarily about mentors and teachers, about the ones who show us the way. We do not have a word for when help comes in the other direction.

And maybe it has to be that way. I rebelled against Couture and others who I believed represented the old ways. I thought it was better to forge my own way forward, alone if needed. But when I did, Zola was the one who seemed to understand me best. Another young unknown at the time, but he defended my work—defended it before he knew me. Now Gervex and Roll led the charge for me, along with Guillemet and Vuillefroy. As Duez said, "the youth" threw their weight behind me.

Which is not to say they are children. Roll is thirty-five, a grown man, and Gervex, though he is just twenty-nine, has been a fully mature artist for years. But they are the ones who pled for me. Not my peers, not my fathers.

I could never make sense of the bitterness from Baudelaire all those years ago. At that terrible low time after *Olympia*, when a kind word, a bit of understanding, would have been like balm, he castigated me. *Do you think you are the only artist who has been criticized? Do you think you have more genius than Wagner? You are first only in your mind.*

It was the old saw, the thing the old always say to the young: Who do you think you are? It came from the wellspring of his own bitterness, his own sense of failure. But I did not know that at the time. It seemed like another ugly judgment. Another attack.

It took me a year to be able to look him in the face after that letter. And in another year he was dead. Maybe it was his illness that made him cruel. I can understand that better than any other explanation.

And perhaps I have it all wrong. Maybe it is not about the direction from which support flows, from old to young or vice versa. Maybe it is instead the sense of self-worth and standing of the proponent. Gervex and Roll could champion me because they were assured of their place. Success came early and overwhelmingly to both of them, and it somehow felt right and natural to them to be generous. Yet I think that is also too simplistic. They chose to behave with benevolence and goodwill. It was conscious. Deliberate.

And yet, and yet—people do what they can, don't they? Baudelaire encouraged me to exhibit *Olympia*, and maybe that was all he was meant to do for me. Maybe he was simply provoking me, but he made me overcome my reluctance and fear about showing that painting, and in that sense, he helped me find my fate, for better or for worse. So what if it took sixteen years for success to come? If my way has been rocky, that was not his fault—it was simply the way of the world.

THIS IS HOW I SLEEP: on my belly and side, my pillow cradled in my arms, my left leg extended full-length. I wrap my good foot and ankle around it, like a vine around an old log.

SOLD TWO PAINTINGS TO M. Gauthier-Lathuille: *Oloron Sainte-Marie* and a seascape. I am puzzled by the choices, although no more than usual.

What makes a person buy one painting over another? A combination of taste and purpose, I know. But *Oloron*? Except for the cat licking itself clean, there is nothing charming about it, and it is nearly devoid of color. It is a strange piece, with that wide strip of white running through it and the sole figure on the balcony.

But maybe that is precisely what Gauthier-Lathuille wanted. Something unusual. Many people want a painting that allows them to go on thinking their own thoughts, or that brings something pleasant, like a Renoir does, where everyone and everything is glowing and happy. It would make me crazy to be faced every day with that kind of happiness—I could not live up to it.

And maybe Gauthier-Lathuille could not, either. *Oloron Sainte-Marie* is pensive. Melancholy, even. It gives the spectator room only for a small range of responses. One can say, *I feel exactly as that poor bastard on the balcony feels*, or, *at least I am doing better today than he is*.

Whatever the reason, Gauthier-Lathuille wanted my blacks and whites and grays. Maybe they bring him peace of mind.

MALLARMÉ WROTE—HE WANTS me to illustrate more of Poe's poems, as I did with "The Raven."

"My dear captain," I replied, "though I would love to make this voyage with you, I do not have the strength or the imagination."

Now I am even turning away old friends.

I used the words "strength" and "imagination"—but the problem is both more and less profound than that. What I really mean to say is that I have no interest in drawing or painting anything. Except perhaps cows and bumblebees—

It astounds me that a year ago I wrote several times a week to Isabelle Lemonnier, and decorated my letters to her with watercolor illustrations. That infatuation seems like a lifetime ago and utterly mysterious to me. Though that is the way with love affairs—they occupy your mind wholly for a time, and then they become distant countries where you no longer speak the language and have forgotten all the landmarks.

Versailles   31 JULY 1881

EVENING PRIMROSE GLOWS EVEN on rainy days. Both the
spent and new blossoms give off light. One is the warm gold of metal, the
other—lemons.

I WROTE AGAIN TO Mallarmé and apologized. Told him that if he could wait until I return to Paris, I would do my best to make images that might live up to Poe's poems and his translations.

"You will give me the spirit I need," I told him.

Poets are terrible with their fantastical worlds—it is almost impossible to turn them into images. But I will try. I will also paint Bernstein's young son—he has asked me several times, and I keep putting him off. If I do that, it will not only please him, it will convince S and Eugénie they can stop worrying so much. I can still paint if I need to, even if I do not want to.

S HAD HER HAIR in pigtails today, and she looked the way she did when she was nineteen. She always wore a severe braid when she was teaching, and I could never wait to get her into bed and fray that tight coil. After we had sex, she would be so warm she would tie her hair into loose pigtails, just to get it off her neck.

I think that was a thing Berthe could never forgive in me—that I once loved S.

"I can even understand why you bedded her, why you seduced her," she would say. "But why marry her?"

"She was the mother of my son."

"You could have provided for them in other ways."

Around and around it went. I never bothered to say that if I had not married S, I likely would have married someone else before I ever met her. To Berthe, S was the obstacle.

Even then it seemed ridiculous to me that she used the word "seduce" for what happened, and now it seems more silly still. I was seventeen when I met S, who was nineteen. We were young. Virgins. I thought I was a man at the time—I thought I knew things. But I could have no more seduced a woman than played a symphony.

I think some women cannot accept that there are beauties contrary to their own, or that desire and predilection do not always follow fashion. Could Berthe have accepted Trine or my gypsy girl or the woman with the pocks? I doubt it.

All this flashed through my mind just now when I saw S's hair, and of course I said nothing—I have always said nothing. I just leaned down and kissed the part between the pigtails.

But it occurs to me more and more that I admire women more than I do men. Not that I do not admire my own sex, or at least some individuals—of course I do. But on the whole, I admire women more, and more different types of women, than I do men. And they are, altogether, more deserving of admiration.

One is trained to think of women occupying a different sphere, and they do—the obstacles for them in the world are real. But they move beyond those obstacles all the time, and by all manner of means. And women of all milieus do this: women like Berthe and Eva Gonzalès and Marie Bracquemond, and Cassatt and Bashkirtseff, but also women like Méry and Victorine. They do this in spite of all the obstacles before them.

That is what I should have proposed to the prefect for the decoration of the meeting room at the new Hôtel de Ville—the women of Paris. And yet I am sure the offer would have been interpreted as an appeal to paint a new Marianne. What an outrage would have occurred if, instead of the French ideal, I gave them flower makers and flower sellers, milliners, servers of beer, artists, metal burnishers, dancers, demimondaines, fishwives, concierges, maids, madams, vegetable sellers, lace makers, seamstresses, cooks, madams, hairdressers, ladies-in-waiting, governesses, washerwomen, and artists' models.

THINKING AGAIN OF VUILLEFROY and his cows. I do not know why it took me so long to see it, but he is a direct descendant of Fragonard. All of those white cows and bulls that each of them painted! I thought it was simply bucolic, but now I think there is more to it. There is a great French tradition of cow painting.

The cows across the lane have gotten so used to us that they come to the fence to see us whether Léon is with us with the fife or not. They stand, watching us watch them, and we all just enjoy the others' company. Sometimes I sketch, but as often as not I simply sit in the chair that we leave beside the fence, watching S talk to them and pet their great heads.

Today I petted the cow she calls Demi because it is a bit smaller. The fur? hair? is not soft over the bone of the skull, but there is a plush quality to it all the same. A kind of hard velvet—

As I was rubbing my hand over its head, the cow stuck out its tongue and licked my wrist. It made me laugh.

"They like the taste of us," S said. "We are salty to them."

So I stood there until Demi got tired of me and moved off.

TONIN CAME TO VISIT for the day yesterday, and I told him how bleak I had been feeling this summer.

"And now with Cabaner's death—"

"That was a blessing," he said.

"No, it would have been a blessing if he'd gotten better," I told him. "This was just an ugly inevitability."

We both went silent then, but in a little while, he said, "You know, maybe it is this place that is affecting you. Versailles itself. Thiers had forty thousand brought here to be tried. The misery of the Communards is more than any garden, no matter how grand, can make up for."

"So you're claiming I feel the sorrow of this place?"

"It is a sorrowful place. Especially for a republican like you."

He held forth then about the history of the place, about all the suffering we have witnessed at the hands of men who claim to know the greater good. He was in high style. And yet everything he said was true, and I know I have painted very little here. The desultory garden. Still lifes in the form of my dead rabbit and eagle-owl.

Versailles has been a kind of death sentence for me, too.

I need to get back to Paris. To streets and alleyways and boulevards. To the living.

Versailles   12 SEPTEMBER 1881

WE FOUND OUT WHAT Jicky has been doing in the evenings—he
has lined up eleven dead crickets under the carpet at the back door.

SO HAPPY WAS I to return to Paris that I threw myself a party last night—or at least it felt that way to me. In addition to opening the studio to anyone who would come, I hired a young waiter from a café on Batignolles to serve drinks.

I thought it would be just that, an evening of laughter, gossip, and quick remarks. But then the actress Eugénie-Marie Darlaud came in with her younger sister, and their arrival quickened everyone's pulse in the studio. When the two of them made their way over to me, after thanking Mlle Darlaud for visiting, I asked if they would pose for a quick sketch.

"Well, Anne may if she likes," Eugénie-Marie said, laughing. "I think I would like some champagne."

The younger sister looked down at her dress, which was much simpler than her sibling's, and said, "What, just like this?"

"You are charming as you are," I told her.

And as soon as Jeanne de Marsy—for that is Anne's new stage name—took her place on my stool, things began to happen. People altered their stances and lowered their voices in order to better watch this young woman. It was not just because I was drawing her, either—I work all the time on such nights, and people do not pay such attention. There was something unusual about Mlle de Marsy.

It is partly her face—she has an unusual profile—but it is more than just her looks. Someone would call out a question or comment, and she would answer prettily in a word or two, never breaking her pose. The longer she sat, the more her eyes seemed to shine. She radiated some kind of magic, and the air in the studio fairly crackled with it.

I worked quickly with my pastels—the main thing was to get her wide-set eyes beneath the brim of the hat and the tendrils of hair. When I added a single black line beneath the peach of her mouth for the chin, I heard someone say, over my shoulder, "That's it."

"That was a delightful," Bracquemond told me after I put down the pastel and thanked my model for her time. "We have thoroughly missed you."

"Ever the magician with pastels," Chabrier said. "You owe me my portrait yet. I hope you still have the interest."

"I have the interest, my friend," I told him. "Come next week at your convenience. I am ready to work."

I acted as if it were all just part of the evening, but today I only have to glance at the pastel to know it was more.

I am on to something in that face.

I have an idea for a portrait for which I am convinced she is the key and the catalyst. Or rather, I have had the idea for a while, but now I see a way to it. I mean to paint Jeanne de Marsy as springtime itself, in a painting filled with flowers and blue sky—brilliant lapis-lazuli blue.

A YES FROM MLLE DE MARSY. I have it in a note. I wasted no time in writing, and she wasted none in responding.

I said "preliminary sketches" in my letter to her, but I know. I know. She is *Spring.*

"I was a child and she was a child,
In this kingdom by the sea."

First love, early love—Poe's poem is an ode to it, but it holds no interest for me. I have no interest in virgins or love between "children." But Mallarmé asked for the illustrations, so I will do them out of affection for him.

I had my first love and my early loves, but now all of it seems a lifetime ago, and a fable anyway. Why do we so often celebrate the virginal? I have been guilty of it myself. Where is age in all of this? Agency?

I think Méry has been my only genuine adult love. A woman I walked toward knowingly, understanding the full extent of her power—and my own. There has been discovery with her, and delight at new pleasures, but no ridiculous declarations, no impossible promises—just friendship. I do not worry about her when she is away from me, never feel sick in my stomach over choices I made with her or because of her.

I started some little things at Versailles for this project of Mallarmé's. I thought maybe they were too general, but they are by the sea, by a great, dark northern sea, and I am determined to make them work. I promised my captain I would do the work and I will, but I intend to discharge the job as quickly as possible. I have other pots on the fire.

"I HAVE DRESSES," Mlle de Marsy said when I told her I wanted to be able to choose her frock for the painting. "They aren't all so plain as the one I wore to your studio the other night."

"And I am sure you look beautiful in all of them," I told her. "But I still need to choose."

It was clear from her face that my flattery wasn't enough to convince—it never is with intelligent people.

"The truth is, the dress is a kind of prop, mademoiselle," I explained. "I need for it to conform strictly to my vision for the painting. Your dress and your hat and your gloves all must function together."

That time, she nodded.

So today at Mme Derot's shop, we chose fabric for a day dress, white dotted with sprigs of cornflowers, bluebells, and yellow rosebuds. There will be lace at the sleeves and the neck—I know that much—but I left the rest of the details to Mme Derrot and Mlle de Marsy, who speak the language of dresses fluently. I do not need to dictate everything.

LA DAME VIROT the milliner has a shop window on the street, of course, but her atelier and the room where one goes to pick out ribbon and stuffs is up a flight of stairs. By the time I realized I would have to climb them if I were to be involved in picking out Mlle de Marsy's hat, I could not turn back. But I made Mlle de Marsy go ahead of me up the flight so we would not walk up together.

"I want to make a quick sketch," I told her, gesturing to the display in the window. "I'll join you shortly."

Once she was safely upstairs, I began the long ascent with my cane, my numb foot, and a knee that will no longer bend. Each step took tremendous effort, and the whole climb took much longer than it should have. At the top, I stood on the final step for a moment, holding the rail and collecting myself.

When I moved off that step and into the workroom, I thought perhaps, just perhaps, I had made it.

I was wrong.

As soon as I entered, Mme Virot took one look at me and scurried off to get a chair—a chair that pride would not let me take in that roomful of women. I did not want to appear to be a cripple, an impotent.

If she had not drawn attention to me, I might have found a chair on my own and sunk down into it. But after such an overt display and all the exclamations of concern, I had to reject all of it—not only the solicitousness but also the chair. So I remained standing the entire time. As if it were a natural thing, as if I were a healthy man.

The only concession I made to my pain was to grasp

tightly the back of the chair with one hand and my cane with the other so that I might hold myself up and remove all weight from my bad leg. So that was how I watched Mlle de Marsy model several different styles of hats. When it came time to look at different colors of flowers to adorn the hat, I moved to the counter and leaned heavily on that.

I give myself credit—I maintained my smiling face throughout. And a part of me was delighted by the long table, the scraps of fabric, the bits of ribbon and silk flowers everywhere, Mme Virot sweeping off to grab another bit of something, Mlle de Marsy's happiness. Even in my pain there was pleasure.

Now a day of bed rest to pay for it all.

I WILL NOT WRITE about the fantastical images this morning's dream contained—most were strange symbols, and they already feel faded. What I choose to remember clearly is the peace with which I woke.

I have been in pain and I will be in pain—it is my state, and I accept it. What I can no longer accept is my self-loathing.

It wastes valuable energy and time to castigate myself or this poor shell I live in. It is a strange indulgence, and one that bring only more suffering. So just as I no longer spend time describing the varieties or details of my pain, I can no longer regard myself as the enemy. I can no longer refer to myself as a cripple, a legless wonder, an impotent— not even in my mind. It brings me too low.

I must work with what I have.

> *The last entries were on separate sheets of paper*
> *and not part of the notebook proper. —A. Sosset*

WE DO NOT HAVE the frock yet, though Mme Derot has promised to finish as soon as possible, but today I did the first sketches of Mlle de Marsy using the hat and the gloves, which are made of suede and feature twenty-five buttons.

"I even remembered to bring my glove hook," she told me as she pulled a soft gauntlet over a hand and began to work, button by button.

I watched the delicate silver tip of the hook slip in and out of the suede, saw the concentration in her face—and the whole thing seemed as intimate as watching someone put on a corset.

"Without so many buttons, the fit would not be as nice," she told me, eyes down on her task.

I had to force myself to look away so it would not seem as if I were watching her dress.

"YOU KNOW, I REALLY wanted to be Jane de Marsy, but everyone prefers Jeanne. I understand—Jane confuses people. They wonder if I'm English when they hear it. But I like it better. I like the English *J*. I like the way it sounds, the way it feels in my mouth when I say it. Like a bite of a plum. I don't know why I think that. But I'm a different person when I'm Jane. I'm still myself, but I'm simpler, somehow. More straightforward."

Idle conversation as she poses. Roaming thoughts. Confidences. Secrets that unfold over days.

THE PARASOL MLLE DE MARSY chose is too yellow, at least for the painting. When I told her that, she seemed crestfallen.

"I was careful in choosing," she said. "I thought it would go well with the dress and the gloves."

"It's nothing. I will adjust the color on the canvas."

We passed some time in silence, and then she said, "I'm sure they would let me exchange it for another."

"It isn't necessary. For life, for strolling on the street, you chose the perfect parasol. But I don't want it to overwhelm the painting."

In a little while, I could see all the concern disappear from her face. Her shoulders lowered almost imperceptibly—though perceptibly to me.

"You mean the painting would become too much about the parasol."

"That is exactly what I mean."

And the air in the studio went from troubled to peaceful again.

RECEIVED A YES FROM the railway company to make studies of a locomotive with an engineer and fireman—it seems a good idea for a painting of "the belly of Paris." On the train back from Versailles, no one could have worked harder than the fireman of our train, who was blackened by his work, except where rivulets of sweat washed his face. Such men are the real heroes of the city.

"It will be a far cry from this," Tonin said tonight when I showed him the letter, smiling as he gestured to the painting of Jeanne de Marsy on the easel.

"Exactly. It will do me good."

We all have our strengths and weaknesses, but I do not want to become like my beloved Vuillefroy, painting cows to the exclusion of all else—I do not want to become a painter of pretty things alone. I need to be able to paint all of the city, beautiful or dirty, artful or happenstance. What was the thing Baudelaire said all those years ago, about modernity? About being grand and poetic in our boots and ties? If anyone was poetic, is was the chauffeur on that locomotive. Filthy face, wielding that short-handled shovel, a blue bandanna "tie" around his neck, he was one of the proudest men I ever saw.

IF JEANNE DE MARSY is *Spring* of course Méry is *Autumn*—and she told me today she is not offended by the designation.

"I know I am no longer seventeen, Édouard. In some ways it is a relief to be past that time."

"You don't miss being Venus on the half shell? All of Paris at your beck and call?"

"I miss pieces of it. The good times. Not the heartaches. Paris almost swallowed me whole."

She has told me different things about her life—the childhood in Nancy that was not a childhood, the "botched" abortion she had when she was nineteen. But each time she finished telling such a story, she'd say, "We all of us have our scars, don't we?"

"You are the reason I am attempting this seasons project, you know," I told her.

"I thought you got the idea from Alfred Stevens. Or your little woman friend, Mlle Morisot. Didn't she paint women as summer and winter?"

"Well, if you put it that way, it was Tonin who suggested it. But I mean the moment I really imagined being able to do the thing came from you. You in that tawny coat from Worth."

"You like that coat, don't you?"

"When you wear it you look as if you've come straight from the forest."

The whole time we were talking, I was sketching. I never know if sketching her is work or not—we do so much talking that it seems like a visit. And when we do visit, when we have our assignations, I usually end up drawing her, too.

LOAFER WALKING DOWN THE street with his girl, dipping a shoulder with each step, leaning back with hands in his pockets, and her looping her arm through his.

He rolls down the street so pleased with himself, with her, with the world.

ANOTHER PASTEL OF MÉRY today, this time in a filmy veil—I think that makes five. Even if I do not paint *Autumn* until I finish *Spring*, I want to draw these pastels now. It always helps if I have two things in the works, if I have two stones to turn over in my mind. They rub and click together, tumbling and sparking.

This is the sketchiest of all the pastels, and the most dreamlike. That is why I like it. But I do not think I should use this pose for *Autumn*. If I want to pair the portrait of Mèry with *Spring*, I will need a true profile, and this one is a three-quarter face. And that is exactly the problem with such planned pairings—what works for one must work for the other. While a profile of Jeanne de Marsy is flattering to her because of her nose, it is less so for Mèry, but individuality must be abandoned.

Or maybe I have it all wrong. Maybe I should paint Méry exactly as I want to, and let the feelings of the paintings speak. The titles, and exhibiting them side by side, will indicate the two works belong together.

Time to walk away for now. Time to rest.

ONE ISSUE IS PERFECTLY clear today. The charm of the sketch of Méry in her filmy veil comes in part from the pastels, from the medium itself. *It cannot be replicated in oil.*

What is the answer is to pairing *Spring* with *Autumn*? I do not yet know.

EPHRUSSI STOPPED BY TODAY, I think to pick up his Hokusai octopus as anything—I was remiss in returning the print to him. Yet before he even took off his coat, he wanted to know all about my plans for *Spring*, which is up on an easel.

"Her profile is perfect," he said. "The nose—I've never seen anything so economical and so original."

"I don't know," I said. "Stevens painted women as each of the seasons a couple of years ago."

"I hardly think this is like his work, Édouard."

"I am sure some will think I took the idea from him. But you might as well color in a photograph if you are going to paint like that. Why, one could take the canvas to a fashion house for sewing patterns to be made. I will not turn Jeanne de Marsy into a mannequin."

When I looked away from my canvas and at Ephrussi, I saw he was smiling, arms crossed over his chest.

"Who ever said you would?" he asked me.

GAMBETTA HAS NAMED TONIN the minister of arts in his newly formed cabinet. He reddened as he told me, and I knew then the appointment had moved him—deeply.

"I wanted to confide in you before," he said. "But it was not official. In truth, I was not sure this entire ministry would come to pass."

"Is support that weak?"

"Gambetta is attempting to unite people who have no interest in uniting," he said. "So I plan to move quickly. I will nominate you immediately for your cross. You will be a chevalier of the Legion of Honor."

I did not say anything—I stood there like a fool. When I began to ask something, Tonin put up his hand.

"I am not singling you out—your name will be one of several," he said. "If I do not have the freedom to do this, then there is no power in my appointment."

We sat in silence for a moment, and then I said, "It sounds like yet another battle, my friend."

"What isn't a battle?"

But I am afraid to believe in the thing. Not out of lack of trust in Tonin or faith in Gambetta's leadership. I mean I am afraid to believe in the possibility. When I was younger I would have. And I would have bristled that recognition had been so long coming, or indulged in secret delight that I had proved the naysayers wrong.

But I am not the man I was. I am not the man I was at thirty, or even forty. And yet, to be a chevalier—

A chevalier.

I TOLD MYSELF I would not believe in the thing, would not so much as think about it—but I do think about it. I wonder what obstacles will beset my nomination, and what pitfalls lie ahead.

This title will not allow me to forge new bonds with powerful people. Those who support me now have always done so, and those who have been against me will remain so.

The title will not open doors for me. Even if it does, I will be unable to walk through them. This disease has taken my strength.

But I have some strength still. And I want the thing.

"NOT MANET!"

That is what the president of France himself declared when Tonin read his list of nominations for the cross of the Legion of Honor. But for once, Tonin was not alone in championing me—Gambetta came to his aid, and to mine.

"Gambetta, you know he is shaped like a barrel. Well, he turned with his full weight to face Grévy and said, 'Monsieur, it is well understood that each minister has the right to name individuals for the Legion of Honor within his arena. Not even you, the president of the republic, may contradict that.' It was a full repudiation, and a public one."

Tonin relayed the news with such gusto, I had to take pleasure in its telling. Yet the whole episode underscores how fragile my nomination is, and how strongly it will rankle some.

"If this does go through, you and Gambetta are the only reasons," I said.

"Listen, Édouard, I proposed it. It was upheld by Gambetta. It will be celebrated by hundreds, and toasted over and over again by your friends in the grand and not-so-grand places of Paris. You will have to accept this victory."

I nodded. I did not have any words, so I grasped him by the hand.

"It is your victory, too," I told him.

"No. It belongs to you, and you alone. But, old man, I wish you could have seen Grévy's face when Gambetta reprimanded him," he said, shaking his head. "When he realized how thoroughly he had been trounced, he gave a very tight-lipped smile."

"Grévy smiled gravely?"

We laughed then at the bad pun like the aging schoolboys that we are.

A GREEN TENDRIL OF an idea is growing.

It is the tendril of a thistle come up beside a stone at Les Halles, nourished by fish guts and offal, tougher than stone itself, and impossible to root out.

If I can find a way to paint it—if I can find the strength to paint it.

Paris   29 NOVEMBER 1881

A BLACK OCTOPUS NIGHT.

ALMOST AN ENTIRE WEEK LOST. My left foot alternates from numb to boiling, over and over, while the right is on a low simmer always. I do not feel like calling Sireday—I cannot bear to see his long face and hear the same pronouncements.

So instead I sip Tardieu's liqueur, the same recipe I used when my foot first began to pinch and ache. All these years later, and I still do not increase the proportion of laudanum. It relieves as it always has, but it also makes me morose, stupid, and unable to shit. I need only think of Baudelaire and I want to pitch the bottle. My breath smells so much of the cinnamon and cloves of the Sydenham's that one would think I started drinking the Christmas punch early.

I have an appointment the day after tomorrow. Not with Sireday—I am going behind his back to see someone else. I hope it is not a fool's errand. I think I am an open mark, ripe for any charlatan, but what is the alternative?

Liqueur Ambroise Tardieu

Heat 20 centiliters of alcohol to 36 degrees.
Add 6 drops of oil of peppermint & 6 grams of Sydenham's
   laudanum.

Separately, heat 30 centiliters distilled water and dissolve
   100 grams of sugar within.
Mix thoroughly.

DR. PIERRE POTAIN. Tall and slender, though without the hunch that afflicts so many tall men. Cadaverous and somewhat dour, and yet what joy he brought me!

He thought my problems might be from gonococcal arthritis, which is a dreadful diagnosis for anyone else but a good one for me. And perhaps I should not believe him at all—his specialty is the heart, after all—but he has great faith that I will experience improvement with his ergot concoction. And so I choose to have faith in him and in it. I take the mixture as religiously as an altar boy takes Communion: a quarter of a gram daily, increasing to a half gram if necessary, and alternating with nitrate of silver.

As Potain explained it, the ergot decreases blood supply and makes the muscles less susceptible to tremors. The tissue somehow is "smoothed out."

"One must not overuse it," Potain told me sternly, his eyes piercing mine from under his brow. "I cannot stress that enough. But I believe it will help your condition."

Potain's face—I wish I could have made a study of it. His cheeks are so hollow they show his anatomy: the gathering of muscle over each cheekbone and hollow triangle beneath. He must have felt me studying him, for as he was writing the script, he suddenly turned those all-seeing eyes on me and said, "You observe me as carefully as a doctor does a patient, Monsieur Manet."

"The architecture of your face delights me, Doctor."

He smiled at the lunacy of my comment. I mean smiled with his entire face, not just a measly, pursed-mouth grin but an all-encompassing, open-mouth-in-surprise-and-delight smile that extended up into his eyes. That single expression transformed him and convinced me of his character. At that moment I realized I felt something I have not felt in months, not since the days of the salamander in the garden.

Hope. A tiny bit, but I felt it all the same.

Of course, I will not say a word about this new medication to Sireday—he would be furious. No, that is not fair. He would voice his concern and speak earnestly to me about chasing cures. But that, too, is unbearable. Seeing him these days is like seeing the undertaker.

HOPE—I KEEP SAYING the word, marveling at it.

Modern and world-weary, we think we are beyond it. Too wise, too jaded, we think we are past such a thing. We know what the world is, what men do to other men, and to women, and what anyone may do to a child. We have seen horrors. Executioners in uniforms. Poverty. Illness.

Then It comes with its threadlike feet and delicate wings. It drinks our sweat and tears, and once again we believe things are possible.

I will not squander this opportunity, this grand gesture Tonin has set in motion. I will find a way to paint this idea I have been tending in my heart. I commit to it here, in these pages, in the presence of whatever gods and goddesses still exist.

I will paint a mural of the women of Paris *one canvas at a time.*

AT THE FOLIES-BERGÈRE

An approach is made. She waits because it is her job to wait, but the thing begins long before he reaches the bar. He has surveyed the possibilities and made a choice—or perhaps he has not. Perhaps it is all up to chance.

She is pretty—all the barmaids are pretty—but there is also something severe about this one's face. Something stark.

He asks for a drink and she complies. When she hands him his glass, he uses the opportunity to say more. His comments are exploratory. Thinly veiled, or joking, or brusque. From my angle I can see his hand gesturing a bit, his head moving.

She listens without expression, or with nothing but the most neutral of expressions. She does not smile or nod or incline her head. She takes in his words, there in the noise of the place, with all of life playing out around them—with me looking on.

I am too far away to hear, and his back is to me, but from his spine and shoulders and the gesturing hand, I understand. He flirts, he flatters, he cajoles. Younger than I am but not young, he must now work or pay for what once came freely. It takes time, more and more time, and he has paid only for the minutes of conversation it takes to purchase a drink.

I have to look away. Down to this page. A failed voyeur, I do not want to see how the moment plays out.

When I look up again, after the time it takes to write this, she is waiting on her next customer. He is gone, lost in the crowd, dismissed entirely.

As am I—

THE DAY PEOPLE NO longer desire you—you know for a long time that it is coming. Then it arrives and it is still shocking. Someone may still touch you out of love or affection, or kindness, or duty. But not desire. The ridiculous flirtation with Isabelle Lemonnier last year taught me that. But while it may take only once to learn the lesson, you go on feeling it.

Last night, though I was an observer only, it somehow seemed as if I were the one who had approached the barmaid with the stark and beautiful face and waited for her judgment.

But let me say it more plainly still, because last night I knew—knew wholly and completely.

I will never approach a woman again.

Paris 13 DECEMBER 1881

I—

I WENT BACK, BACK to that riot of sound and noise and life.

I went because it was my job to go back if I want to paint my vision.

This time I was armed with a purpose: to find the barmaid from the other night. But she was not there. In her place, a professional beauty with a golden wig and powdered face.

She worked the counter skillfully, pouring drinks, chatting with customers, laughing, smiling. When she took money from someone's hand, she dipped her head and nodded, sometimes even closing her eyes for the briefest of moments. She was very pretty to watch. And even when I thought I saw her energy flagging, she kept her features in check, regarding everything with a pleasant expression, as if she were waiting happily to fulfill the next request. The only gesture that belied her performance was the way she grasped her own wrists in front of her. That was the only place where she let fatigue or nervousness show. In the whole time I watched her, I saw her turn away from the floor only twice—once to stifle a yawn and once to wipe her nose very carefully, so as not to disturb the red of her lips.

She was masterful.

But even though I drew her repeatedly, and no matter how much attention I lavished on the glowing mass of her hair, she never came alive on the page. Her artful dark brows and the crimson of her mouth were not enough to animate her face.

All I could think of was the savage barmaid of the other night. With her stiff shoulders and unyielding expression, she was an awkward amateur in comparison to the seasoned beauty in front of me. But she is the one I want.

The blonde—I felt disloyal, somehow, sitting and analyzing her even as I drew her. She fascinated me, and part of me did fall in love with her a little. She was beautiful, though in the end I could not tell.

Sometimes one is not hungry for sugar—

AT ANY OTHER TIME I would have kept quiet about the idea, even with Tonin—I do not believe in talking about things before I do them. But when he came by today, I somehow wanted to include him in this new plan. I think I wanted to show him that my best is not behind me, and that the cross he sought for me will not be solely for what I did in the past, but also for what I might yet do.

"This barmaid is wrong, I know it. But I know one who will make it right," I said, showing him the study I made of the pleasant blonde at the Folies-Bergère. "I have to go back and find her."

"It will be a masterwork, my friend," he said after I stopped talking, and after he had a good long look at the study and a few of my sketches. "Like a gathering of forces."

"Yes, I will go back to the bar with my long sack, gathering berries and barmaids."

I wanted to make him smile again, and he obliged me. Some of the fatigue and tension in his face eased for a moment.

But he is right—the work will be a culmination. And I have been gathering bits for it for a lifetime.

MLLE SUZON TONNERRE. That is her name.

Last night I made a full show of it—sitting where she might see me working, letting her observe me. I did not want her to believe I was like all the others. Only after a long time of drawing did I approach the bar. With pencil marks still on my fingers, I introduced myself and asked her if she could come to pose for me.

"For an appropriate sum, of course," I said. "Is twenty francs acceptable for a day?"

At first I received the same cool glance she gave to her suitor the other night, but then something broke in her features. I saw the beginning of movement in her mouth before I heard her reply, *Yes, it is.*

An answer to my question. No more, no less. No easy flirtation, no idle talk, no willing smile.

And yet, and yet. To stand there within that gaze and let her observe you is a conversation in itself. Within a moment you are pierced, all sound and motion stops around you, and you stand, bleeding out—

Paris

A HISS AND A MOAN—even her name is enigmatic. Suzon.

"I COME FROM ÎLE DE GROIX, m'sieur. I lived there until I was thirteen, when my mother and little sisters and I moved to Lorient. That's where my mother's people were from. After my father and brother died at sea, she wanted to get off the island.

"Why, they were tuna fishermen, like everyone else on Groix. They died in a storm that sunk seven boats and killed fifty-three men. Yes, I miss my father. For a long time I could remember what his voice sounded like, but now I can't.

"I miss everything about the island. In the summer I liked to walk over the country roads and hear all the crickets ticking and scratching in the heat. At one spot, the cove was so sheltered and quiet you could go into water that was almost like a bath. Other days, when I felt wild, I would walk to the cliffs and watch the waves crashing. I think I am a bit wild, like my name—Tonnerre.

"I do not know if I would like to go back. Maybe after I have made my way in the world.

"No one has ever asked me such things here. In Paris, I mean. I think you must be a bit unusual, m'sieur. Is it rude to say that? I knew you were unusual when I saw you at the Folies, drawing in your carnet. Usually if someone asks me something at work, it is one of the bosses and it is all about work. Or the things customers ask me—there's that, too.

"Well, you asked me for something, too, but what you want is different. Simple, if you don't mind me saying. You want me to stand here. It is like a vacation, if you really want to know, it isn't work at all. I wonder that you pay me for it. But it is my time, and that is something, isn't it? Even so, I appreciate it."

. . .

The way I have written it here makes it seem a monologue, as if it came out in a blurt. But it did not. These details spooled out over hours. Most of our time in the studio was spent in silence. I worried at first that I was not entertaining enough, or that Mlle Tonnerre was quiet because she felt ill at ease—and then I stopped thinking about it. Stopped thinking of anything but the sketches in front of me. And I realized I was able to do so because of the profound composure of Suzon Tonnerre.

To be quiet like that is a power most people do not have until they are old. Yet she possesses it already. She must have learned it on Groix, from all that time watching the sea. Or maybe that deep stillness has been in her all along. Léon was solemn as a baby and as a boy, and as a man he is still careful—pensive, even. Some people are what they are immediately. Their core never changes.

But how is it that she has appeared precisely as I needed her? It is not simply her face that I needed, either—it is her whole being. I had some sense of her coolness and self-possession when I saw her the first night at the Folies-Bergère—and yet I was absolutely unprepared for the experience of being with her today. In her presence I felt the wildness of everything she talked about, the whole of the Atlantic. There is something untamed within her, and how she keeps ahold of it in this city is a mystery I hope I never solve.

Paris   26 DECEMBER 1881

DAYS LOST TO THE HOLIDAY. I would rather work.

THE OFFICIAL LIST OF those to be decorated is published: knights, officers, commanders, grand officers, and the Grand Cross. As a chevalier, I get a red ribbon with a laurel wreath and five white "swallows' tails." Just as I felt a sense of something finally being attained with the Salon award, I feel this chevalier's cross is some grand conclusion, an ultimate fruition.

My pleasure at the thing is genuine. Sincere and untarnished.

So why did I reply as I did to Chesneau's letter? I long ago forgave him for what he said about *Olympia*—he has been a supporter longer than any other critic. But when he mentioned that Count Nieuwerkerke also sent his congratulations on my title, the sentiment quickly became unbearable.

"Thank you for your kind words, my dear Chesneau," I wrote, "but as for the Count, you may tell him that he could have decorated me himself years ago. He would have made my fortune for me. Now it is too late to make up for twenty years of failure."

My anger came out of its hiding place like a snake. For once I said what I thought of someone in power, and my words tasted bitter. The idea that old men become peaceful or philosophical—what shit. One learns to endure, that is all.

THE DAY BEFORE THE new year, and here I am, in my studio. The only celebration I want to attend is this one where I am the host and only guest. Not out of cantankerousness, either—I came here to think and diagnose a problem.

First I laid out all the sketches I made of Mlle Tonnerre the other day, and then I studied them, individually at first, then taking a step back, surveying the whole. They pleased me because Mlle Tonnerre pleases me, and yet something seemed amiss about every drawing. The fault was not with Mlle Tonnerre—I needed only look at the sketch I showed to Tonin of the first insipid barmaid to know that I have the right model for this work.

But something still displeased me.

I did not know what I was searching for when I walked away from the table. And yet somehow I must have known, for I went almost directly to stand in front of one painting.

The Execution of Maximilian.

The canvas that Émilie Ambre took with her so confidently to America. That Beauplan refused to show further after its poor performance in New York. That next to no one in France has seen because of the censors. That hangs once again on my wall, where it will no doubt stay long after I am gone because it depicts state-sanctioned murder.

I stared at the blue-black of the soldiers' uniforms and the white of their sashes, and my eye went from detail to detail, all so familiar I was no longer sure I could even perceive them. I tilted my head upward to study the witnesses at the wall, and then found myself wanting to squat down so I could better examine the bare dirt of the foreground—and that was when it came to me.

I need to take up more space with Mlle Tonnerre. She needs to take up more space.

The soldiers in *Maximilian* are almost life-size. And at eight feet high by ten feet wide, the painting makes physical demands. To take it all in, you must step back. To see details, you must crane your neck and stoop—and then do it all over again.

That is what I want for Mlle Tonnerre.

As soon as the thought formed in my mind, I heard a voice inside my head—my own voice. *Of course, of course. You wanted to paint a mural of the women of Paris, and you still do.* A mural, not a portrait. Not a little painting of a sugarcoated barmaid. Not a variation of Jeanne de Marsy in her pretty dress and bonnet.

The realization so stunned me that I sat down on the divan to let it wash over me. And to write all of this out—

If I could, I would paint Mlle Tonnerre at the Folies-Bergère the same size I painted the execution. That is beyond me now. I cannot stretch and bend, I cannot balance on a ladder, I cannot nimbly climb about the surface of a canvas as I once did.

But I must push myself. If I want this new work to be more, I must make it more. I must paint as large as I can.

JEANNE DE MARSY FROM Bordeaux, Renoir from Capri—so many friends have written to me about my decoration. Extravagant with their love and praise, their words strengthen and brace me, like a tonic or sturdy cane.

And yet, and yet—the only thing that matters right now is that I keep working. Today I sketched out a rough study on a sheet, 95 by 130 centimeters, about the size of a size-60 canvas. I fear if I make it any larger, I will not be able to complete it. Every decision is made with that in mind, and I hoard my energy as carefully as a field mouse hoards seeds in winter.

I am going to have Léon and Aristide drag the divan back out here from the dragonfly room so I do not have as far to go to it when I need a rest. Then, with two chairs of different heights and the adjustable easel, I should be able to get through most of the day sitting down, even with this expanse of canvas.

Even so.

GEORGES JEANNIOT SAW THE lot of it yesterday when he came by—my "bar" made from a plank, complete with booze bottles and flowers, Mlle Tonnerre in her uniform, standing behind. I shook his hand from my chair, and he was gracious enough to slip into the scene he found, sitting behind me quietly until I felt able to stop for a moment and speak.

"I do not wish to take you from your work," he told me. "I'm glad just to see you, and offer my congratulations of your decoration."

"It is a fine thing, but in the end it doesn't change anything," I said, and gestured to the easel. "Not the work."

"No, that is the same. Please, go on with it. It is a pleasure simply to watch you."

He is a painter, so I took him at his word, and I went on as long as I could, until I needed to stretch out on the divan, leg extended. More people had come in then anyway—the place is like a train station these days, filled with well-wishers and gawkers. I enjoy it but also know I do not have the strength for it. I could feel some shaking beginning, but I am not sure anyone but Jeanniot noticed—they were busy talking and exclaiming about Goncourt's *La Faustin*, which has just been published.

"I saw him staring at his book through the window at Lefilleul's," Chabrier said.

"I saw him doing the same at Marpon's," a doctor named Robin said, and everyone laughed.

I motioned to Jeanniot to lean close to me and told him, "Come back another day, not a Thursday. It will be quieter and we can talk."

"I will."

Why do simple responses like that, devoid of social niceties, please me so much? Jeanniot's *I will*, or Mlle Tonnerre's *Yes, it is*, the night I asked her to model? Because it takes true sincerity to respond like that, and grace. There is no room for flattery or dishonesty in such a short phrase, and you trust it.

Economy of language, economy of person—there is something there.

WHAT A THING chance is—

A blustery day with light rain that started after I got here to the studio. I thought Mlle Tonnerre might be late but she arrived on time, thoroughly damp because her umbrella broke.

"It was cheap but I thought it would last a little longer," she said. "But one big gust came and blew it inside out."

She spread her coat and scarf on chairs by the stove and then went to take off her hat at the mirror. That was when I saw. She must have felt me staring, because she said, "I know. I am soaked like a soup."

The fashionable curls at her forehead had gotten the worst—they were straight and sticking to her skin. Suddenly she did not look at all like a tempting barmaid or the fashionable young woman I drew the first day.

"You look like a girl from Groix with your hair like that," I told her.

"Don't laugh at me," she said, and began to towel off her bangs with her handkerchief, which got soaked immediately—so I gave her mine

"I'm not laughing," I told her. "I like to see the girl from Groix."

She would not look at me for a while but went on rubbing at her hair, trying to dry it. Then, after she had picked at everything and arranged her bangs as best she could, she turned to look at me.

"I would never go to work like this, m'sieur. The bosses would fire me if I did. My hair is too plain. I already know I don't have the knack of smiling—I have been told that. I have to work to look the part."

Maybe if she had not told me about her family, maybe if I did not know her story, I would not have thought what I did. But I did know her story. She was a fatherless girl from Groix, who liked to watch the wild waves crash, and who came to Paris to make her way.

"Mademoiselle Tonnerre, this is how I would like to paint you. With your bangs straight and your hair pulled back."

"I'm supposed to make myself up for the Folies."

"But this is not the Folies, mademoiselle. This is a painting."

And then she got flustered and did not know what to say. And I felt bad about that. But I need the girl from Groix in the painting. It is how it needs to be.

AS SHE PUT ON her wraps yesterday she made me remember Victorine. How many times I watched V dress, only to strip her down again because watching her dress would so arouse me that I would not let her leave until we lay on the divan once more.

I was hungry for her all the time.

Part of me is in love with Mlle Tonnerre in a similar way. Everything from her silences to her stories intrigues me, and I am curious about her physically. I know what her hair smells like and the particular way her collarbones jut out at the base of her throat and how her dress pulls across her shoulder blades. But the only way I have touched her is when I have taken her hand or arm, and anyone else would laugh at the way I have fantasized about her, all on the basis of how the back of her arm, just above her elbow, feels against my fingertips and in my hand when I find a reason to touch her there. There is a tiny bit off fullness in the skin, and I daydream about taking it in my mouth and sucking on it until it bruises—

BEARD AND MUSTACHE still smell of Méry.

BARROIL SENT A CRATE of tangerines to me here at the studio—
an absolute extravagance as far as I am concerned. In his note, he said,
"You know I loved your painting of the girl serving beer. I am sorry for
all the trouble."

It is not his fault his wife disapproved of his original choice of art-
work. I received a box of Marseille sunshine in exchange for my trouble, so
it was worth it. I will ask S to hunt up a pretty dish for the tangerines, and
some will go onto Mlle Tonnerre's made-up bar, at least until we eat them.

Yellow and orange, yellow and orange. Victorine is the one who told
me I always find a way to give those colors to the paintings I love best—

GAMBETTA HAS FALLEN. It took just sixty-six days.

"I didn't understand the thing was that tenuous," I told Tonin.

"It was over almost as soon as it started," he said, looking tired.

EUGÉNE STOPPED BY WHEN I was scraping off an area of the bar painting in order to redo it.

"How many times have you painted that section?"

"I don't know," I said. "Several."

"You can overwork a thing, you know."

"Yes, Eugéne, I do know that."

"You need to think of your health."

"That is what I am thinking of," I told him. "This does me better than any medicine. It is the reason I get up in the morning."

I think he chalks it up as another of my delusions. But you must be deluded to make art. You must believe so much in the thing that is in your head, and your head only, that you put aside everything else in order to bring it to life for others to see.

I AM SHOCKED BUT not surprised.

A group has formed to harass the seventeen Salon jurors who voted to award me my medal last year. They sent an anonymous screed to all those eligible to vote on this year's jurors, naming the seventeen who voted in favor of my award and imploring everyone not to reward my supporters with reelection. Even now, when it should be too late, the hate I engender is fresh and strong.

I heard about it from Duret, who said, "I cannot believe the mean-spiritedness of the thing."

I can. The second-class medal was one thing, but now that I received the cross, how that must stick in the craw of my detractors.

I know Duret wanted to apprise me, but what can I do? I cannot fight the thing. The letter has been sent, the rumor mill started. I can only go on working on this year's submissions and trust that my fellow painters will make the decision they see fit.

How strange that this notebook has become my confidant for so many things. I look back at the entries from the beginning, when I had no idea what to put in the pages, or at the drawings I put in here—little records of the days, which I am glad to have now. But if someone were to read the entire thing, I think they would wonder why I persisted. Not with this notebook—I mean why I went on painting at all.

In some ways, my work has brought as much pain as pleasure.

I have had only the most limited success, and that success has almost always been accompanied by controversy. Even now, when it should be too late to matter, some feel they must threaten not only me but those who support me.

But I never did quit. I went on. Why?

Because I believed I painted important things. Real things. And I painted in a way that made sense to me.

Of course, anyone may claim that he believes in what he does, and anyone may believe his own pronouncements. But I mean something more than that. I mean my eyes told me my work was sound. My eyes told me that my art was an important and sincere representation of this world and this life. I did not go on painting because I believed in myself—many days I did not. I went on painting because I believed in what I *saw*.

THE SECOND DAY WITHOUT my cane. Is it the beginning of remission that Potain talked about, or just a moment of respite? Someone dangling grapes in front of me that I cannot quite reach?

To walk without my third leg, what a pleasure!

THOSE FEW DAYS WERE an exception. I am shaky as ever today. My leg kicks out as if on a spring.

So be it. I will work all day sitting down.

SIREDAY CAME TO SEE me today because I have been avoiding him.

"You never stay away so long, Édouard," he said. "I fear something is afoot."

"That is a horrible pun," I told him.

He looked chagrined, but nothing would put him off his task, which was to determine what I have been doing these past two months.

"I only use laudanum when I have to," I said. "You know I don't like the stupidity it induces."

"It is safer than some things you might do," he said then, as if he knew exactly what prescription I had been taking.

"Look," I told him, getting up from my chair so he could see me move. "I spend as much time as I can sitting. Resting. But I must have some kind of ability to work."

More urging from him, further denials from me. And then he left. But he must have run into Tonin out on the street, because when T came in, he said immediately, "He is worried about you."

"He's my doctor. It is his job to worry."

"He wants me to talk to you about the dangers of drugs he doesn't prescribe."

I haven't told anyone except Méry about the ergot. I thought someone should know, but she is the only one I can trust not to lecture me. But people see things.

"I am doing what I need to do, Tonin."

It is hard to describe the sensation brought about by the ergot. I still have pain, still have trouble moving. But things are muffled somehow on this drug. If it allows me to come here most days, I will take it no matter what Sireday or anyone else says.

s told me at breakfast this morning that Sireday had come to see her as well. "He is concerned that you are working too much."

"So you are the one who contacted him," I said.

She looked at me for a long time, and then she got up from her chair and came and stood in front of me.

"I did not," she told me. "I've seen the bottle, but I know better than to try to intervene."

I felt stupid then for my tone. "Sorry," I said. "I won't go on using the concoction forever."

"You don't have to. It has already done you damage."

She stood looking down at me in my chair, and I finally let myself meet her eyes.

"These get deeper each day," she said, and moved her hand to my forehead, where the grooves have deepened. Her thumb ran over the skin there, but there is no amount of pressing that will smooth things out—the creases are permanent.

"I have to squint more and more," I said. "It's affecting my sight."

She did not say anything but went on watching me, and then she moved her cool palm to my cheek.

"I know," she said. "I see you holding things closer and closer."

"I just want to delay the inevitable a while longer," I said. Then I grabbed her hand and kissed the center of her palm, where all the lines cross. Kissed it over and over.

MÉRY IS THERE IN her yellow gloves, and Jeanne de Marsy in the dress and hat she wore to the studio that first night. I even put in a version of Victorine in her green boots. Though I made her into a trapeze performer, I do not think she would mind.

The only truly recognizable man is Gaston La Touche, with his voluminous mustache and silly little beard.

But you only see those details long after you take in Suzon, Suzon of the straight bangs, stung mouth, and twin-starred eyes.

"Why did you make me look like that?" she asked today—probably the last day I will need her to pose.

It sounds like a challenge when I write it here, but it was not. It was just a question. So I answered it.

"Because that is how you appear to me," I told her.

"I must have been thinking of home that day. I didn't know you could see it."

"I cannot see your thoughts. You know that."

"Yes," she said. "But still."

I wanted to tell her that her expression was an amalgamation of all the days we spent together. But I did not say anything more because I did not want to break the profound quietness that she carries with her. It is a cloak that surrounds her. At that moment, it was spread over me, too. So we just went on looking at the painting. Her standing, and me in my chair.

IF MÉRY IS NOT sending flowers, it is her chambermaid Elisa, tasked with bringing me a piece of fruit or candy.

"You work too hard, m'sieur," Elisa tells me every time she finds me at my easel. "Why don't you lie down and put your feet up? Take a rest."

"I need to keep working, mademoiselle," I said today after I ate the coconut candy she brought me. "And I need to paint you one day."

"Go on, then," she said, laughing.

Sometimes I do sit and rest, and listen to her tell stories of her mistress. The stories are all kind about Méry, but not her suitors. Today she told me about Evans the dentist, and how he always smells strongly of cologne.

"Why, it must be like kissing a perfume bottle," Elisa said, and we laughed meanly.

A BAR AT THE Folies-Bergère is done. *Not a brushstroke more*, as Tonin says. I looked at it with Mlle Tonnerre on her last day, with Chabrier the other day, and Tonin many times—but today I looked alone. I tried to take a step back from the thing and ended up pulling my chair here and there so I could sit and look at it. Really look. Of course, it is impossible to have any perspective on it, and yet I must, because the entire tableau seems strange to me, as if I'd painted it in a fever or a dream.

Maybe that is the ergot. But it is also how I always feel at the end of something big and complex. By the time I paint the final bits, the earlier pieces are weeks old. But I think I feel more than that this time.

I love:

~ The size of the thing.

~ Mlle Tonnerre's forearms, bare, framed by lace and a bracelet.

~ The green boots of the trapeze artist.

~ The swirl of the background where one can sense sound and light and motion—and then, at the center . . . stillness.

~ The way Mlle Tonnerre holds herself against La Touche's entreaty.

~ Her eyes, which are hazel-gray-green with bits of light, but also mauve, in the shadows beneath her eyes.

~ Her gaze itself, a gaze that takes you in and does not judge. A gaze that is hers, but also a place in which you see Groix, the ocean, Paris, and time itself—time you spend willingly in front of her.

Sitting here in the drafts of the studio, by myself, I can almost see the thing I did.

I THOUGHT OF STOPPING the ergot. Thought and thought, and for a few days I did decrease the dose.

Then I decided not to bother.

What damage there is, is done. My fingers feel numb—I grip the pen woodenly. But my fingers have felt numb off and on for some time. I gripped things as I could these past two months, I imagined my little opalescent octopuses, and I went on painting. I saw the thing to completion, the largest canvas I could manage, *une toile de soixante*. And when I look over to *Bar*, it all seems worthwhile—

NOTES ON PAINTING

Oh, my friends, you think color is the most exciting thing—and it is. But it is not the only element that creates drama. Perspective, composition, and scale are equally important.

Your eye will be drawn to the central figure of Mlle Tonnerre—but also distracted by the mirrored reflections to the right, and the sea of figures to the left. The ongoing tension, the constant tug on your senses. *Where should I look now?*

Mlle Tonnerre will form a triangle at the center, with her angled arms as its sides. She is the center of the composition, which is itself a form of triptych, an altarpiece of modern life, if you will.

I mean for the painting to be viewed at eye level, or slightly above, because I want you to come face-to-face with Mlle Tonnerre.

The scale is crucial. The size of the canvas immediately communicates that this woman in the black dress of a *serveuse* is significant enough to support a large-scale painting. This barmaid has a story to tell, and it is the story not only of the Folies-Bergère, it is the story of Paris.

Which is why there must be some *mystery* in each "panel" of the triptych. Who is the elegant woman in long yellow gloves on the left? And the dangling legs of the figure on the trapeze—to whom do they belong? What kind of woman performs in midair *on* a bar, *in* a bar? And who is the mysterious figure on the far right? What is he asking for? A beverage or the barmaid's favors? Is he kind and flirtatious, or brusque and ashamed?

Most importantly, is *he* the focus of the barmaid's gaze, or are you? Are you a person who seeks out every distraction offered in this riotous circus of life and love? Are you a participant or merely a spectator? For, by your mere presence in front of this painting, you have indicated that you are a voyeur of modern life in all its forms.

Friends, are you like me?

TURNED IN NOT ONLY *A Bar at the Folies-Bergère*, but also *Spring*—my wild girl from Groix and the ultimate Parisienne. They are gone. Submitted to the Salon *hors concourse*, automatically to be shown, with no jury to cajole or please. Fifty years old and I have finally been deemed to be worthy.

I could have sent them earlier, but I did not. I did not want to be parted from *Bar*. There is always a loss when one comes to the end of a work like that.

I DREW A PASTEL of Méry's Viennese friend Mlle Irma Brunner, and all three of us are pleased with it.

When Mlle Brunner was posing, I told her and Méry about the day Mme Albazzi stopped by the studio and carried off George Moore to go riding in the Bois de Boulogne.

"Before he got in her carriage, he told me she was a mistress for Attila. He was quite taken with her," I said.

"He will put that in his memoirs," Méry said. "He will describe her *chose* in detail."

"Who would you be a mistress for in history, Méry?" Mlle Brunner asked.

"She has already played Venus on the stage, Mademoiselle Brunner," I said.

"Besides being lover to the god Mars, then."

"Not Louis XIV, I can tell you," Méry said. "I heard he smelled like a goat."

They went on laughing, and I went on sketching and sketching.

THE SPACE IN STUDIO occupied by *Bar* seems not just empty but barren. That work fed me a vital fluid for weeks. Now I both miss the painting and fear for its reception.

What will people do when faced with the gaze of Suzon Tonnerre?

Victorine destroyed the Salon in *Olympia* with her stare. To see a woman's eyes and breasts and outline of her sex all at the *same time*—it was a challenge to which no one could rise. Even when Courbet painted his *Origin of the World*, one did not see his model's face, only her magnificent mound.

But Mlle Tonnerre is clothed. This time I have asked less of people. Will people look at her and see a woman with the whole of the ocean in her gaze? Or will she confound them with her frankness as Trine did?

People say they want realism, but most are not ready for it. And if I am honest, I am not ready to embrace realism, true realism, either. Yes, I can paint a woman's direct gaze, her body, and at least what I can see of her spirit. But I cannot look at my own left leg and foot.

WHITE LILACS FROM MÉRY. Forced, grown out in Belleville—they cost her dearly, I know. I brush against them with my nose and mouth, like a bumblebee.

THIRTEEN OF MY SUPPORTERS were elected again to the Salon jury, so the efforts of the anonymous group to decimate my champions largely failed. But their letter did poison the well for Bin, Gervex, Guillaumet, and Lévy—they have all lost their positions as jurors.

It pains me. They have been ostracized simply for their connection to me.

Gervex is strong—he will laugh and say to hell with it all. But I hope the others do not regret standing up for me. I thanked them last year, but I am not sure they understood the extent of the hatred for my art and for me. Now they have been dragged down into the miasma, too.

TODAY IN THE STUDIO I overheard someone saying, "Nailed to his chair."

I know people talk, but at least they could wait until I am out of earshot to say such things.

FAURE CAME TO THE studio today to tell me he will pay 11,000 fr. for four paintings, including my old *Music in the Tuileries.*

"I would do this even if I did not want you to paint my portrait," he said. "Though I hope it will free you from other commissions so that we may begin."

Faure—it is hard to withstand such a force. Still, I told him I would have to wait until next month. I do not have the patience for the thing right now, or the energy. It is one thing to sit and sketch pastels of Méry and her friends, but it is another thing entirely to attempt an oil of a demanding man.

Why do some people feel the need to fill the air with so many words? They do not give you time to think about the last thing they said before bombarding you with more.

MÉRY TODAY IN the studio:

"You know, it is something of an achievement to be a woman with my lifestyle and not have children. But that was the silver lining to my abortion—it took away the possibility. That butchery was a blessing, really. I knew early on I didn't want a child."

No one escapes this life.

I AM SURPRISED—IT SEEMS my fretting was for nothing. The first Salon reviews are out, and it appears that even the old bear Wolff is offering an olive branch of sorts.

Though he made sure to begin by saying he would never be entirely in accord with me, and that my art was not for everyone, he acknowledged that *Spring* created a "ravishing impression" and that *Bar at the Folies-Bergère* was "a curious arrangement." But I suppose all I can hope for from Wolff is faint praise. At least he had the grace to say that I did not learn my art in museums, but that I instead "seized it" directly from nature.

And today in *Voltaire*, Alexandre Hepp writes, "I have always thought that first place prizes are not *given*: they are, instead, *taken*. And Manet, artist and boxer, painter and battler, has taken his place by force . . ."

Boxer and battler—if only he had seen me painting *A Bar at the Folies-Bergère* from my chair with my foot propped up, cane close by.

Paris   4 MAY 1882

I DO NOT KNOW what to say. In today's *Gaulois*, there are more than
a hundred lines by Louis de Fourcaud on my works. And yes, I am sure
there are more than one hundred—I counted twice.

He writes prettily about *Spring*, calling it "exquisite," but he saves his
real salvos for *Bar*, saying it is the more significant of the two works.

> It is one of Manet's best paintings. It is the most original, the
> freshest, the most harmonious of all he has produced... The
> young barmaid talks with a man we cannot see except by reflec-
> tion; a gold pendant on a black ribbon adorns her neck; between
> her breasts a corsage nestles; her blond bangs reach to her eye-
> brows. Do you know anything more ingenious as a composition,
> more spiritual, more expressive? Fellow artists have long done
> justice to Manet, and the day will come when he is recognized
> as a French Goya, or possessing the same merits as Frans Hals.

A French Goya—it made me laugh out loud. After years of reading
the ugliest kinds of things about my work, I have trained myself to dis-
trust the whole industry. And yet to read someone's words about a thing
you love, and to understand from those words that he loves it, too—

TONIN CAME BY TO tell me about the ceremony he helped preside over, along with Castagnary, at the new École des Beaux-Arts—the new home of the largest display of Gustave Courbet's works ever seen.

"Of course President Grévy was there in all his finery," he said, "and he could not have spoken more glowingly about Courbet. The same Courbet imprisoned for his role in the Commune, which was never more than a trumped-up lie. The same Courbet excluded from the Salon because of his 'pornographic' paintings. The same man the government hounded into Switzerland. And now after his death he is lauded."

"It's just revisionism, Tonin," I said. "The winds of favor and fortune change, and so does public opinion."

"The irony is dizzying," he told me. "No wonder you get vertigo."

It was such a good line, and he said it with such exasperation, that I reached out to shake his hand.

REVIEWS STILL OF *BAR* AND *SPRING*, including one by Armand Silvestre:

"His figure of *Spring* has the charm of the most beautiful Japanese images but with a distinctly Parisian perfume. As for *Bar at the Folies-Bergère*, there has never been anything more alive. Its tones sparkle and astonish. It is absolutely regal."

I am grateful, truly, and moved, but I would give every word to wake up without pain. Does this blasted disease not know that I am finally acceptable in the public's eye? Can it not give me a moment's peace to enjoy my late and small success?

Paris 6 JUNE 1882

ELISA CAME BY TODAY with a little bouquet of white cockles, bluebells, and goat's beard. As precious to me in its own way as Méry's lilacs—

I SHOULD STILL BE celebrating but do not have the energy. I sleep as much as Jicky.

IN OUR HOUSE RENTED from Eugène Labiche. A cream-colored box with two stories, only one of which I will see. The garden is smaller than last year's at Versailles. But it has a piano for S, a robinia tree out front, and a little stone path in the garden. It is all I can walk anyway—the shortest of paths.

Most importantly, the house boasts an indoor toilet. That is really what clinched the deal.

MARGINALLY BETTER TODAY, so I sat outside in the shade, sketching the tree. The girl who works in the kitchen and who carried out a chair for me said it was beautiful when it was flowering.

"People use it in beignets," she told me.

"What do they use in donuts?" I asked, since I was only half listening to her.

"The flowers of the trees, monsieur. They dip them in batter and fry them. My mother makes them very well."

"What do they taste like?"

"A little bit like honey, a little like oranges. At least that is what people say. I have not eaten too many oranges myself."

"Robinia donuts," I said, looking up at the tree.

"We call it acacia, monsieur."

She went back inside then to help S in the house, and I sat and thought about beignets d'acacia for the rest of the morning.

I AM OUT IN the garden, in the shade of the acacia. A bird is calling, the same few notes over and over. It is just the song the bird was born to, so why does it strike me as sad? Perhaps it is the notes themselves, or the fact that no other bird calls out an answer.

I believe this is the first day I have fully been *here* in this small garden of this nondescript house—I have resisted accepting the place and everything it represents. But today I accept the close horizon, the foreshortened view. There are bumblebees here, and birds, and a smattering of flowers. Even diminished as Nature is in this place, it still has the power to quiet my mind for the first time in weeks—since the day I pulled out a chair and sat looking at *A Bar at the Folies-Bergère* in my studio.

Firsts are easy to recognize. You know when the first snow falls in a winter, or when you see the first lilac in spring. You know the first time you kiss a woman, the first time you make love to her. You know precisely in time and pay attention accordingly. What is much harder is to know the *last* of things. Those you do not recognize until time has passed. Sometimes, by the time you know for certain, so much time has intervened that details escape you. Or, worse, you did not know you were losing, so you did not pay attention.

But that day in the studio with *Bar*, studying it, I did know. I recognized a last time. I accepted it, even though I have not been able to bring myself to think of it again. But here in the shade of this acacia, let me write the thing I knew that day in the studio and have been afraid to think about clearly since, but which colors all my thoughts, and whose truth I can no longer avoid, since avoiding has not brought peace:

I will not paint again, not as I painted *A Bar at the Folies-Bergère*. It took all I had.

And now I sound old and morose. I blame that bird with his sad song.

FOR SOME REASON, the gossip columnist at *L'Évenément* felt compelled to include a note in yesterday's paper about my health, saying I was "quite stricken," and that he hoped my illness was not "very grave." God forbid I should fall out of the public eye for even a month!

I do not know who was behind the thing—there are so many culprits from which to choose. So now I will have to send a note debunking the thing, and creating some plausible lie for my "numerous friends," as the paper calls those who are supposedly concerned about me. I will say I twisted my ankle—that will suffice for that rag. But I know they will publish anything I send because it will help them fan the flames a little longer.

A gossip column has to be mean-spirited—that is the point of the thing. But I truthfully do not know what the preoccupation with me is about. Surely there must be some more interesting scandal that "M. Manet's health"?

RAIN AGAIN. ONE CAN only read so much, so after breakfast I set up shop here inside the dining room, next to the window. I suppose I could have gone to hell with myself and simply painted from my bed.

I better not joke about it—that day may yet come.

Today's model was a very accommodating basket of strawberries. Mlle Marotte piled them artfully on some pretty greens she found in her mother's garden. They formed a perfect pyramid until I told her to help me eat some off the top.

"The point looks unnatural," I said.

As we nibbled and neatly piled the green tops in our hands, Mlle Marotte said, "They are perfectly ripe, m'sieur. They really should be eaten today."

"Then I will have to work fast, won't I?" I told her.

I can see she was fascinated by all of it—the paint and brushes and all the mess I was making. Which is just as well, since I always need someone to help with the cleaning up.

There are worse things than painting indoors with strawberry juice on my fingers.

THE TRUTH IS THAT some days it is even hard for me to write in here, my hand shakes so. It took all my effort to make a legible note to Méry yesterday.

If I say any more I will become maudlin.

TODAY I ASKED MLLE MAROTTE to bring me peaches from the market, some that were a few days out.

"So not perfectly ripe and not ready to eat," she said.

"Exactly. I want to be able to paint them for a couple of days."

"Very well, m'sieur. I will see what I can do," she told me importantly.

Eugénie must have overheard the whole thing, because at lunch she said, "I see you have a new assistant."

"She is very able, Mother."

"I, for one, am glad," S said. "If Louise didn't want to run your errands, I would have to do it."

And all Eugénie could do was sniff.

SONG OF THE PEACHES

Yes we are radiant,
like little suns,
or even the moon in some
months—we enchant
even at a distance.
Up close, our soft skin
so like hers that you think
when you bite, for an instant
that she's there with you,
but it's only us blushing.
Do not let the velvet fool
you. We are luscious,
with hard hearts—

Rueil

I THINK I MUST have sounded worse than usual in that last letter to Tonin—today he sent a bunch of roses here to S and me.

At least I will have those to paint now.

AFTER SOME MOMENTS OF watching S smiling to herself over coffee and bread this morning, I asked, "What is it?"

"I woke up with a little ball of yarn in my nightgown," she said. "A little toy I made for Jicky. He brings it to bed sometimes, and last night it must have got caught up in my chemise."

BERTHE AND EUGÈNE HAVE come for a couple of days. Even after all this time I find it difficult to be around them. I think Berthe feels the same way. She behaves woodenly, I am tongue-tied, and it is up to Eugéne and S to keep things afloat.

Though it pained me, this morning I sat outside for some time, sketching Bibi. She looked charming in a dark red bonnet Berthe had her dressed in, and it was easier to do that than find something for all of us to talk about.

"Have you begun to think about what you will submit to next year's Salon?" Eugène asked me at lunch.

"I have not," I said. "I simply try to get through the days."

Though I did not mean for it to kill all conversation, that was the effect—or maybe it would have happened anyway. People try to behave normally around me, but I know they find my state alarming, and it is difficult to hide how much difficulty I have in walking even a dozen steps. When I am here with just S and Eugénie, or when Léon comes on the weekends, we can all pretend I am holding my own. But if someone new comes, even family, the charade is exposed.

Except it isn't a charade, is it? This is how I walk, this is how I live— how we all live, because I have drawn everyone into my drama. I lurch and hobble and grimace, I spend hours of the day with my legs up on the divan, watching it rain.

Reuil

PAINTING APPLES AGAIN. Yesterday there were four, and today there are only three because I ate one. Each painting a bit smaller than the last.

I THINK I DO have a regret in my life. I think I sometimes trusted others' opinions of me more than I trusted my own. Yet who among those that criticized knew me as well as I know myself? And who among them did I trust as much as I trusted myself?

Yet I often believed their judgment of me to be more accurate than my own judgment of myself. I believed their criticisms contained some form of truth. Now I know they did not. They were simple and petty attacks, like rocks thrown by schoolboys, or insults and taunts made to impress others with their cleverness.

This all seems like a terrible miscalculation on my part.

In the end it did not matter—I went on working. In the end it was my own voice I listened to. But I wish I had been gentler with myself. I wish I had taken better care of myself.

These gray rainy days give me too much time to think.

THIS MORNING I SAW a sparrow sitting on the fence with a dragon-fly in its mouth. It had captured the thing, but the wings were too wide for it to swallow. When the bird opened its mouth, I thought it might let its prize go, but it tilted its head back and somehow worked the dragonfly down a bit and then a bit more. It did that about six times until the wings disappeared.

The sparrow sat on the fence for a moment and then it flew off. All done with breakfast.

I WRITE THIS PLAINLY.

Bathing last night, I ran my right foot over and under my left foot as I always do—and my toe caught on something. I felt something begin to throb dully in my bad foot, and then the water in the tub began to fill with blood. Little billowing plumes of red—

I tried to bend my knee to see what happened, but I have so little mobility in that leg that I could not get the right angle to see where the blood was coming from. I cannot even see my own goddamn foot. So I called for S. She came and looked and blotted the blood and water away with a towel, and she told me as much with her expression as any words might.

I have a hole in my foot, the size of S's thumb, where the tissue has given way. From a blister or an ulcer—

"Why didn't you tell me this was happening?" S asked, but as soon as she said the words, she answered her own question.

"You didn't feel it, did you?" she said.

"I am not sure," I said, which is the truth. My hobbling has been even more painful recently, but at other times my foot feels dead.

She sent off a letter to Sireday today, but I already know what his response will be. I will begin packing now—

THE WILL IS STANDARD in some ways—of course S is my legatee. But we also had to take steps to make our wishes clear about Léon without naming him as my son. When I asked S if she wanted to set things right, finally, she said, "It is too late for that."

"It is not too late to recognize him as my son," I told her.

"It is too late for him to be raised as your son."

She is right—we cannot get those years back when he might have benefitted in some way from the Manet name. We should have ended the lie after my father died, but S did not want to lose the reputation she had created for herself, the legitimacy of her place. So Léon will legally remain who he has always been: my brother-in-law. The fiction will be maintained. And if the charade is tragic to me, I know it is equally tragic to S, and to Léon himself.

Sireday did not mince words or offer false hope. At this point, the thing is to get the ulcer healed, and that requires me to stay off the foot entirely.

"As for ergot, if you are taking it, you must stop at once," Sireday told me. "It will only decrease blood supply to your foot."

I nodded when he said it—the only acknowledgment I have made about my visit to Potain.

Between the trip home and the visits to Sireday and the notary, I am exhausted. Perhaps things will look less bleak when I have had a chance to rest. But right now—right now I do not see the way forward—

Paris

MÉRY SENT A BOUQUET—roses, carnations, and pansies. When Léon comes home from work, I am going to ask him to help me rig up an easel here in the dining room, just as we had in the house Reuil.

When S saw Méry's name on the card, she took a moment and then said, "Well, she cannot very well come to the house, can she?" But she put the flowers in a great glass-footed vase for me anyway.

FLOWERS AGAIN, THIS TIME from Duret. He saw what I was doing the other day when he came by, so he wrote, "You probably need a fresh bouquet by now."

The roses themselves are breathtaking, especially the yellow, which is so various in its colors it goes from gold to pale cream with just a touch of crimson near the center. But the surprise is how beautiful the stems themselves look in S's heavy glass vase. They, too, are variegated in color, and the water reflects their surfaces like a prism, as well as the tablecloth. In the morning light, the water itself looks violet-blue. Or do I just imagine I see that color everywhere?

Storm-cloud-gray for the background, dove for the tablecloth, and for the water—cornflower-blue.

MESMERIZED EQUALLY BY THE golden reflections sunlight made on a glass vase filled with water as by the flowers themselves standing in the vase. Glass, water, reflections—I am becoming a painter of that which is transparent. Our eyes perceive glass and water readily, but to render such transparency with oil paint, well, that is the challenge. One has to make something see-through out of something that is opaque.

That kind of trick—it is why people love the woman in the magnificent blue dress that Ingres painted. He managed to portray satin, producing not just the folds and wrinkles of the fabric but also its mirror-like sheen, with layers of paint. We all love the magic of it, the trick he made for our eyes, and we delight in it each time we see it, even though we know the trick is coming, even though we know it is a trick.

"Painting Glass, Water, and other See-Through Things, a Treatise," by E. Manet, author of "Violet All Around Us: Painting Air."

SOME FLOWERS NEED a black background, which of course is never really black but maroonish black, like Jicky, or greenish black, like Jean Piolet's crow. Other flowers need a gray background, which is never simply gray but can be leaden or charcoal-like, or a hundred colors in between. If I am in this dark place, this black and gray place, let me be here. Let me see it fully, and love what there is to love.

Baleine gris, temps gris, loup marin gris, travail au gris, éminence grise.

Le petit gris, meaning either a snail or a squirrel or a paintbrush made from the hairs of said gray squirrel.

Grisette.

"IMPROVING. SCARRING OVER NICELY." That is what Sireday told me.

"Can I begin walking again?"

"No. Perhaps a little, here in the apartment."

He must have seen the look on my face, because in another moment he told me, "You must limit your movement greatly from now on, Édouard. Otherwise the bones in your foot will continue deteriorating. It is the nature of Charcot foot."

"Should I go and see Charcot himself?"

"You can if you want. I doubt he will tell you anything different."

"Then how exactly have things 'improved'?"

"You no longer have an open wound. The skin involved is healing. The ulcer did not reach the bone. You do not have an infection. You do not have a fever. Blood is still flowing in the tissues of your foot—"

"You have made your point," I said, and waved my hand. Hearing him enumerate it all made me sick to my stomach. I know I offended him with that question about whether or not I should go to see Charcot, but how is one supposed to take such news?

I am not supposed to walk again. The idea that I have "improved" is an illusion. Now it simply means that the precipitous slide has been temporarily halted.

Later, when Eugénie asked me how the visit had gone, I told her in detail. Then I felt an ass for upsetting her.

"YOU SAID SIREDAY GAVE you leave to hobble about a bit, right?" Léon asked. "Then I don't see what the problem is. You can go to your studio and hobble around a bit there as easily as you can here."

"How will I get there?" I said like a petulant old man. "I am not supposed to walk any more than is necessary."

"Take a carriage. There are carriages in Paris, you know."

"From one street to the next? The driver would turn me out for such a trifling fare."

"Not if you pay him well."

"I should be able to walk the distance."

"If you go on thinking that way, you will stay right here in this apartment," he told me.

I do not know when he learned to talk to me that way—as if I were the child in need of instruction. But he was fully right.

"I will ask Aristide to find you a driver for a couple times a week. Do you want to try that?"

"Yes," I told him, grudgingly. Gratefully.

So that is the plan for now: arrange in advance the days I want to go to the studio, and have a carriage pick me up at the door.

"What if I am not well enough to go the days I have planned to go?" I said finally. One last attempt to be right.

"Then you'll pay the driver anyway and send him on his way. And try again another time."

I wonder sometimes at Léon's patience. He works at his job and then comes home and helps me with anything I might ask of him, from moving furniture to arranging to ship off paintings to constructing a bar out of an old wooden plank. My pragmatic son, who trades stocks and commodities and deals with every part of life I have always been uninterested in, has figured out a way to set me free, not only from this apartment but my own foolishness. *Take a carriage around the corner? Yes, that is what Manet does now. Nothing can keep him from his work.*

WORD MUST BE OUT that I am back in my studio—last night there was quite a turnout. Maybe people wanted to see if the rumors about my health were true, or maybe they were simply glad to see me, though I never got up from my chair until Léon came to fetch me.

A journalist named Maizeroy made an entrance wearing a top hat and black greatcoat and leading a black Barbet—one's eyes did not know whether to settle on the dog or the man, and both were impressive for their fur. Not only was Maizeroy sporting a full beard and mustache, his top hat was beaver and his coat had a sable collar. The dog's messy curls endeared him to everyone present, and no one could keep their hands from his fur.

"He looks as if he were wearing Turkish harem pants," I heard a woman exclaim, and I laughed out loud at the description, for it was as accurate as it was humorous.

The whole thing captivated me so much I got out a canvas and my pastel box, even though I had told myself an hour ago that I was done working for the day. I got Maizeroy's face and mien down quickly enough, but the dog was another matter—he was here, there, any- and everywhere, running from hand to hand, and overexcited from all the attention.

"You have to forgive him," Maizeroy said. "He is young and still being trained."

"Can you hold him by his leash?" I asked. "If I get the gist of him down, it will suffice."

So Maizeroy held him, but the dog still wouldn't stop moving entirely, so I had to satisfy myself with a general outline.

"Perhaps you can bring him back on your own another day," I said. "He might be calmer if there were fewer people around."

The chagrin on Maizeroy's face was almost comical as he admitted to everyone within earshot, "He is not my dog. I borrowed him from an army officer and I have to return him."

"You wanted the dog to help you meet women, did you, René?" someone joked, and the room laughed.

He took it all in stride. I think he was more embarrassed to admit that he borrowed the dog than he was about his purpose in borrowing him. Such men live to be noticed, to cause a fuss wherever they go, and Maizeroy was happy to garner such solid attention for an evening.

MLLE SAGUEZ, THE DAUGHTER of the bookseller on rue de Moscou, will come to pose for me this Friday.

I had the driver stop by M. Saguez's store today with the express purpose of asking him if he would allow his daughter to model for me.

"I remember her from the days I came by your store in the past," I explained. "I believe she would be perfect for a new painting I wish to begin."

He was so eager to assist he went upstairs immediately and brought Mlle Lucy back with him to the carriage so we could speak directly and make plans.

She was exactly as I remembered her: Reserved, polite, a dark brunette with a wide face and full lips that make a slight moue. Her features and coloring are strong enough to stand up to the manner in which I want to paint her—as a true *amazone* and circus equestrienne in a black riding habit, holding a crop.

I think the idea has been with me since I saw Émilie Loisset perform at the Cirque d'Hiver, but it was not until the other night with Maizeroy that I understood how I could paint such a portrait here at the studio. One of the women, wanting to tease Maizeroy, put on his top hat—and she immediately became a circus rider. The hat transformed her. Unadorned as she was by any bow or other feminine decoration, it made the same striking silhouette as the hat Émilie Loisset wore when she rode, and I felt suddenly as if I were seeing her again—even though I read accounts of her funeral this spring.

If I cannot paint a genuine performer on her horse, I can at least depict a model in the costume. And I will paint my mural of the modern women of Paris, one canvas at a time.

I COMPLETED A STUDY of Faure.

It tired me to listen to him. It tired me to talk to him. As much as was possible, I let my mind wander off—to think of my *amazone* in her riding gear, to think of the bouquet I have waiting at home for me.

At the end of the session, Faure said, "I think you must be feeling better, my friend. I know you are in pain, but you soldier on. I admire that. Not only do you go on working, you have a pleasant look on your face."

If only he knew it had nothing to do with him!

Paris   1 JANUARY 1883

BONNE ANNÉE TO ALL. To me, too.

MY CHRISTMAS PRESENT FROM MÉRY—a tiny box with strips of ivory in the lid. One side of the strip poses a question, a riddle. When you insert the strip into an opening in the box, the answer to the question is revealed. What is constant? *Change.* What solves problems? *A walk.* What cures? *Sleep.* What calms? *Water.* What lives longest? *Hope.*

But my favorite is this:

What consoles?

Time.

FAURE HAS DONE IT AGAIN. I made two separate studies, and a nearly complete version of a portrait where the beard is silky and the eye has a depth that engages—and he has rejected it all. He told me it was not "suitable."

I would be angry if I had the time or energy.

"I have the time and the energy," Tonin said when I told him. "I would like to slap his stupid, arrogant face."

"He doesn't like the bags beneath his eyes or his bald, shining head."

"Doesn't he have a mirror?" Tonin said. "You can only paint what raw material is there."

"He can't accept that he's growing old."

As he was tucking everything away for me, I said, "Well, Faure did pay me for the four paintings he claimed in the spring, plus one other."

"What did he buy?"

"*In the Conservatory, The Tuileries*, that one of Léon eating a pear, the portrait of Rochefort, and one of the house in Reuil."

"For how much?"

"Eleven thousand."

"That is not enough," Tonin said, making the choking sound he makes when he is exasperated. "He should have paid you that for *In the Conservatory* alone."

"He would never pay that much for a painting of mine. He only buys my stuff because it is cheap and it allows him to think of himself as a patron."

"He's not a patron, he's a vulture," Tonin spit out.

"And tell me this: Why buy Rochefort's portrait? Why does one ass buy the portrait of another ass?"

"Maybe because Rochefort has better hair," he said.

I laughed then to please Tonin, but I am still upset—and not only because I need the money the commission would have brought. I will not get those hours back that I spent on his stupid portrait. Healthy people think nothing of the time and energy they waste because they have it in spades, but Faure also wasted my time.

MÉRY CAME TODAY. I felt desultory, but I made an effort for her. We thought up new questions for the puzzle box she gave me for Christmas.

What lasts forever?

Nothing.

What do we know?

Nothing.

Who loves longest?

Women.

Who loves best?

Women.

So we concluded we would not do very well in the puzzle-box-making business.

YESTERDAY I HAD THREE studies of Mlle Saguez in her riding clothes. Today I have two.

There was a profile of her looking over her shoulder, a frontal half portrait ending at the waist, and a larger portrait, not full-length but nearly so. I showed everything to Pierre Prins, who stopped by the studio to see what I was up to.

"That is my plan for this year's Salon," I said, gesturing to the three works. "I am pressed for time, but I believe I can complete something if I apply myself."

"She makes for a striking figure, Édouard," Prins said. "The subject matter could not be more timely."

He was leaning in close to the smaller of the portraits, hands behind his back, devoting himself entirely to the act of looking. When he backed away from it, he turned to me, and I saw genuine appreciation there, and understanding. He paints only landscapes, only rural subjects, but he is a gentle and truthful painter, and I have always trusted his judgment.

And then suddenly, strangely, it became unbearable to me to pretend I was planning to submit anything.

"That's the only one worth anything," I said, lifting my chin to the half portrait. "Not the rest."

And then I hobbled, for all I can do is hobble, to the cabinet where I keep all the tools for stretching and cutting canvas. I picked up a knife and went to the largest of the studies and slashed the thing from top to bottom. Not through the face—I could not do that. But from the shoulder to the bottom of the canvas.

I know Prins said my name before I cut the thing—I heard him. But he did not try to stop me.

The truth is he could not have stopped me—I told him that after I stood in front of the wrecked canvas for some minutes in silence.

"It was a static composition," I said. "There was no life there. It was a mannequin."

"Sometimes it is best to start over," he said carefully, nodding.

"I need to lie down, Pierre," I told him then, and made my way to the divan to sit. "Please forgive me."

"Of course, of course," he said. "Can I get you anything?"

"A glass of water."

He stayed beside me while I drank it, and then I lay down and closed my eyes. I did not attempt to explain, did not attempt to be polite. I heard him wait a moment, but then he must have understood, because the next thing I heard was him closing the door of the studio.

I got up one more time, painfully, to lock it, and to grab this notebook.

I want no visitors today.

THE CANVAS IS STILL split in two—no fairies have come to repair it.

I think the affair with Faure upset me more than I let on, even to Tonin. You swallow things and swallow things—and then you can swallow no more. When Prins was here, I thought of all the time I had wasted on Faure's portrait—all the time I could have been painting my *amazone*. I did not try to master my emotions once they began, and I let the thing come boiling out of me.

All I know for certain is that the fiction of the Salon has become unbearable to me. I do not believe I have the strength to finish anything for it.

Yet even in my outburst the other day, I showed some restraint. I slashed the weakest and most rudimentary of the studies. If I am able to finish anything, it will be the pose where Mlle Saguez holds the crop like a weapon across her breast, and where her great, dark eyes look out at the world and defy it—

MY BIRTHDAY. Fifty-one years old. I made it here to the studio. My neighbor Dupray came by with his dog.

I TOOK SOME OF Faure's money and made the driver stop at a florist, where I ordered a bouquet of white lilacs to be delivered to Méry, and a bouquet of carnations and clematis for me to take along to S. If the clerk taking my order thought anything of my double request, he had the great sense to keep his face a blank slate.

I do not know how many people Méry has persuaded to send me bouquets, but the vase on the dining room table has rarely been empty. Without those hothouse flowers to paint, days at the apartment would be even more dismal than they are. I do not know how many small flower "portraits" I have done—probably a dozen.

S will comment on the cost, I know, but she will also be pleased about the clematis. They were a favorite of her grandmother's, of Suzanna's, who took care of Léon when he was a baby.

TOCHÉ CAME BY TODAY to see how I was.

"That you can see, my friend," I said as I gestured to my legs. "But one must work to live."

We talked of everything and nothing, including Venice, where we met long ago.

"Do you know, not a week goes by that I do not remember something about that visit," Toché told me. "The regatta we saw, or buying fruit from a boat along some canal in Dorsoduro."

"I remember biting into a pastry that I thought would be peach and it was fish instead. I had to spit the thing out."

Toché laughed and said, "A classic mistake."

"It might have been a very good fish pastry, but I could not stomach it. Not when I wanted peach."

It went that way for some time, with me reclining and chatting idly with him. And when he asked, as everyone always does, what I would be submitting this year, it felt easy to say, "I may have something in the works," and not offer any details. I do not have to explain myself to anyone.

I HAD LÉON DRAG an armchair into the dragonfly room.

"Why? It will not be easy for you to get to if we move it back there."

"No, but once I get there at least I will have a place to rest."

I did not want to admit to him that I miss being in that little room among all the glinting wings.

He moved the chair, and then he walked with me until I was seated in it. He dragged an old ottoman back there, too, so I would have somewhere to rest my leg.

"There. Now you can pretend you are on the riverbank," he told me, so I guess he knew how I felt all along.

THIS IS WHAT I DO: I spend the early part of the morning resting and reading in the apartment.

The carriage comes to pick me up at noon. Then I go to my studio, where I read and I rest.

MÉRY CAME TODAY. She rubbed my neck for me, and my shoulders, and then I brushed her hair.

I AM THINKING AGAIN of trying to finish this portrait of the circus rider. A day or two of solid work and I could finish.

One glove is a muddy mess, and one does not even exist. But it could.

GETTING HERE WAS A worse struggle than usual. Not even my cane is enough to steady me.

The truth is that I need a second cane. The truth is that even my good leg is getting weaker. But so are my hands and arms. It could be that a second cane would not help.

That is the problem with truth. Once you start telling it, you cannot stop.

I WROTE A NOTE to Defeuille today to ask him if he will give me a little instruction in the art of painting miniatures.

"You will find me a capable pupil," I wrote, "and eager to learn."

If it is now a challenge to paint works on even a size-one canvas, perhaps going smaller is the answer. Though I also fear the level of detail required will be beyond me, with my fingers in their current state—

But perhaps this is a whole new arena: the Impressionist miniature. A single flower bud, a glove neatly folded, Méry's swan brooch. The tradition of miniature painting focuses on lifelike precision in painting, but why can it not change, too? Why can't a miniature be like a single breath of the modern?

There is always something to paint, and a way to paint it.

DOWN WITH A BAD fever for the past week, and what Eugénie keeps calling "fulgurating pain," even though the word is "fulminating." I do not have a word for what I felt. For what I feel—

But today I am here. Weak, but here. I sat for some time with the dragonflies, and now I am lying here with this notebook. The Thursday before Easter, so I am not sure if anyone will be out visiting. But the studio is open, and I am glad to be here. And if no one comes, I will still be glad. This space, which once seemed so cavernous and impersonal, now seems familiar and comforting.

On the way, I had the driver stop at the flower stalls on place Moncey for hyacinths. He went himself so I would not have to get out of the carriage, and he brought the pot into the studio for me. The perfume of the three stalks is so strong and fresh it is like spring itself, like an entire bed of hyacinths.

I love all the hothouse bouquets Méry sends, but I am just as happy with these simple flowers in their rough container. I used to think I preferred some flowers over others, but now I do not. Hyacinths, tulips, narcissus—I wish I could paint them all. I love

I SAW HIM THAT day in his studio. Méry sent me with a papier-mâché egg for Easter, filled with sweets. He was sitting on his blue divan with his book, but he put it down as soon as I came in.

"You are my only visitor today," he said.

"Well, you are lucky, then," I told him. "Now you will not have to share your candy."

But the egg was big and he wanted to share it with me. So I got a knife from his worktable, and he held the egg while I cut the strands of lace holding the whole thing closed.

"Even the inside is pretty," he said, for whoever had made the egg lined it with a silvery, printed paper. "Now, what are your favorite candies?"

"I like fruit jellies," I told him.

"Then you pick out those, and I will pick out the ones that I think have coconut."

As we ate, he told me he'd been sick but was doing a bit better.

"Soon it will be warm enough to sit outside," I said. "You will enjoy that, I know."

We visited for a bit and then he asked me, as he always did, to sit long enough for a portrait. I wanted to say no because it made me uncomfortable to think about someone making a picture of me, but I also knew I could not say no. He already looked happier than he had when I came in, and not so tired. So I said yes, and he had me fetch a pad and his pastels.

He sketched and we talked about everything and nothing, just as we always did. The whole room smelled of hyacinth, and we kept on saying how much we loved it, and how it seemed like spring itself. I should have paid closer attention to what he said, I know, but it flustered me to sit there with *his eyes upon me. I know he asked me if I ever missed my family in Nancy, and I told him I did miss my brother.*

He went on drawing with his crayons for some time, and then I saw him stop. He looked tired again, very fatigued. So I took the drawing from him, and put all the pastel crayons away in their box.

"Will you come back tomorrow, Elisa?" he asked me then. "I know it is Good Friday, but if you will sit for me one more time, I can finish this and make you a proper present."

"You do not have to give me a present," I told him. "Seeing you get well would be a present to me."

"You are a flatterer, just like Méry," he said. "So will you come?"

"If you want me to, monsieur," I said.

So we arranged it like that. And I put my hat back on, and my shawl, and I got him a glass of water so he could wash down the candies, and I was about to leave when he took the book from where he had it tucked beside him on the divan.

"I need you to do me a favor, Elisa. I want you to take this notebook."

"Your notebook? Of drawings?"

"Some drawings, yes, but mostly writings. I want you to take it with you."

"Don't you want it?"

He shook his head no and told me, "I do not want my family to have to read it. I jotted things as they came to me, and some of my ramblings might be hurtful to them. I do not want that."

"I can take it if you like," I said. "But I can take it tomorrow just as well."

I saw him think for a moment, but then he handed me the thing anyway. "Bring it back tomorrow," he said. "Maybe I will have something new I want to add."

But that did not happen. The next day, Good Friday, I went back to the studio as I promised him I would, and he was not there.

I told Méry all about what had happened and showed her the notebook, but she would not look at it and she would not take it. "He gave it to you, Elisa, for a reason, and you must be the one to keep it."

I believe the only reason Monsieur Manet gave it to me was that I was the one who showed up that day to see him. It was chance. And yet I also do believe that if I had been a different kind of person, a different sort of woman, he would not have given it to me. So you see both things are true. It was just luck that he chose me, but he did choose me.

And all the terrible things you have heard me tell about his death, they were all true. His foot turned black, gangrene it is called, and the doctors cut it off. But it was all for nothing. He died anyway, at seven in the evening on April 30. That was what the newspapers said at the time, and I have remembered it always. I think everything was too much for him.

Every year after he died, Méry always went to his grave with the first white lilacs of the season. She did that until she died. They were great friends, the two of them. She knew how to be a friend, and so did he.

His art? I'm sure I don't know what to say about that. He painted things that were beautiful, I think. Things that were beautiful to him. But like I told you, he saw the beauty in things that others didn't. Why else would he want to make a picture of me? I think that portrait he started of me was the last thing he ever made. I always wonder what happened to it.

I asked him once after he was so sick why he worked so hard, why he didn't rest more.

"What for, Elisa?" he said. "I might as well use up what I have."

You don't do anything so long as he did unless you love it. He loved to paint and he did it until the end. I think that is the best thing to say.

Fin.

AUTHOR'S NOTES

THE PUZZLE BOX THAT Méry Laurent gave Manet for Christmas in 1882 is based on a gold and ivory box James Salter saw in Paris and described in his memoir *Burning the Days*. The description moved me when I read it, and I asked Jim about it in 1997. He told me he regretted not buying the thing. I would like to think that Jim would not mind that I loaned the box to Manet in this novel.

Perfume lovers will recognize the name Jicky, a Guerlain perfume from 1889 that is still made today. My real-life Jicky is named Nix.

Much of the novel is based on actual events in Manet's life, and many of the characters in these pages are based on real people, like Méry Laurent and Elisa Sosset. When I found Disdéri's *carte de visite* of Méry Laurent for sale on eBay in July 2020, I felt like the Universe had given me a kiss on the forehead; thank you to Bruno Tartarin of Photos Discovery in Arnaville, France, for selling it.

Though much of the novel is based on Manet's life, I used his sketches capriciously. They do not correspond to the dates or events to which I have assigned them.

I pored over a wide variety of sources in both English and French, both primary and secondary, in creating this work of fiction, especially Beth Archer Brombert's *Édouard Manet: Rebel in a Frock Coat*. The recipe for the laudanum liqueur comes directly from Nancy Locke's "Manet's Remedy." If there are mistakes in how I used actual details from Manet's life, they are entirely mine.

Thank you to Jill Bialosky for seeing to it that Manet and Victorine can stay together at W. W. Norton. Thank you to Nicole Aragi for representing me for twenty-two years.

LIST OF IMAGES

[fig. 1] 000: ©RMN-Grand Palais / Art Resource, NY

[fig. 2] 000: From the author's private collection

[fig. 3] 000: ©RMN-Grand Palais / Art Resource, NY

[fig. 4] 000: The Metropolitan Museum of Art, New York:
Rogers Fund, 1921

[fig. 5] 000: From The New York Public Library

[fig. 6] 000: ©RMN-Grand Palais / Art Resource, NY

[fig. 7] 000: ©RMN-Grand Palais / Art Resource, NY

[fig. 8] 000: The Metropolitan Museum of Art, New York:
Harris Brisbane Dick Fund, 1948

[fig. 9] 000: ©RMN-Grand Palais / Art Resource, NY

[fig. 10] 000: ©RMN-Grand Palais / Art Resource, NY

[fig. 11] 000: ©RMN-Grand Palais / Art Resource, NY